DARK GREED

CHARLI CROSS SERIES: BOOK TWO

MARY STONE
DONNA BERDEL

DESCRIPTION

Jealousy is evil. Greed is deadly.

When a young man is found hanging inside a barn, it seems like an open-and-shut suicide. But the boy in question is none other than Bryce Mowery, son and only heir of the richest family in Savannah, and Bryce's father is claiming foul play. Much to her chagrin, Detective Charli Cross is sent to investigate and appease the farm and real estate magnate.

But soon, it's no longer a question of if Bryce was killed, but by who. The Mowerys have made plenty of enemies in town, but why would anyone want to kill the happy-go-lucky playboy? As Charli and her partner Matthew delve deeper into the cutthroat world of land development, the killer is waiting. Not only does he like to play games, but he's covering his tracks . . . and he's developed a taste for murder.

Fast-paced and gripping, Dark Greed is the second book in the Charli Cross series from bestselling author Mary Stone—guar-

anteed to make you reconsider keeping your friends close and your enemies closer.

This book is dedicated to those who have stood on the brink of taking their own lives but didn't. I'm so very, very glad you changed your mind. The world needs you.

1

The heavy shot glass clanked against the granite bar top, causing more than one patron to jump at the sound. Bryce Mowery didn't care. In fact, he enjoyed the attention.

Tequila still burned in Bryce's throat as he waved the bartender down. "I'm done. Close out my tab."

The silver clock on the wall insisted it was eleven-thirty, meaning that last call was only ten minutes away. If it were up to Bryce, he'd be out until two at the earliest, like he'd been the previous summer when visiting friends in Los Angeles.

He needed to get out of Savannah. The laws regarding alcohol sales were merely one of the many reasons he was ready to move.

But how could he leave when he was a king here? A big fish in the small pond, his dad's money got him anything and everything he wanted. Women followed him like eager puppy dogs, and every man in this town wanted to be him. If he ever left, he'd be a nobody, and Bryce hadn't known an existence where attention didn't rain down on him like a spring thunderstorm.

Even now, a petite blonde from across the bar was making eyes at him. Stirring her drink with a skinny red straw, she bit her bottom lip as Bryce's fingers slowly grazed his equally blond hair.

"You know what? I'll cover her tab too. Why not?" Bryce leaned back in his chair, reaching for the bulging wallet in the pocket of his blue jeans.

The bartender's crimson lips frowned. He'd seen her around before, and she had one of those resting bitch faces he liked to avoid.

"Don't you have a girlfriend?" She slid him both receipts but made no effort to hide the judgment in her voice.

"How the hell would you know?" Bryce's disdain for the woman was evident in every syllable.

This was why he didn't come in on weekdays when these nobody bartenders were around. Markus usually worked weekends and treated him like a god the moment he walked through the front door. Why did the bastard have to be sick today?

"You're a Mowery, right? You're Montgomery's son?"

Bryce didn't even try to hide the cocky smile that formed on his face, though the bartender's words dripped with contempt. What could he say? He enjoyed being known, even if it was in infamy.

"Sure am. And whether I am or am not in a relationship is really none of your business, sweetheart. You know my name, so you know Mowery is plastered on every egg carton you've got in the back. Without my family, you wouldn't be able to serve up mediocre omelets on your brunch shifts. You might want to mind yourself, take this card, and pay for whatever that nice young woman ordered."

The credit card flopped on the bar. She took it wordlessly, teeth grinding behind her cheeks, her eyes flashing fire.

That was fine.

Bryce thought nothing of being judged by the working-class trash of this town. At the end of the day, most of them lived in houses the Mowery family name built. His father had his hand in almost all new housing developments in Savannah. Actually, he had his hand in a good chunk of land…from housing to farming to business districts.

And in turn, life was good for Bryce Mowery.

The bartender nearly tossed the card in Bryce's face after ringing him up. Bryce ignored the laborer and simply slid the credit card back into his wallet before leaving a single dollar as a tip. He winked at the seething woman before making his exit. He was already one foot out the door when a voice rang out from over his shoulder.

"Wait!" The skinny blonde was chasing after him, receipt in hand.

"Yes?" Bryce got a better look at her for the first time. She was attractive enough, petite with dimpled cheeks. Personally, Bryce liked his women with more curves.

"Did you pay for my bill?" Her voice had that whiny edge he detested.

"I sure did."

She giggled and twirled a lock of hair around her finger. It was a little too cutesy for Bryce's taste. He liked his flirting subtle. Bryce was a man who enjoyed the chase.

"That was really sweet of you." She stepped closer, looking up at him through her lashes. "You're Bryce, right? Where you headed? We could go back to my place if you don't have any plans."

She was making it too easy for him. "Nah, actually, I've gotta get home." He drew his keys from his pocket, hoping to signal he wasn't interested without having to tell her to go away.

Not that he would have minded doing that, either. He just didn't want to deal with female drama right now.

Maybe he would've been interested if she hadn't come charging over, but for a guy like Bryce, who had women fawning over him daily, desperation was a turnoff.

She dropped her hair, and her eyes went wide. "Wait, you're driving? But aren't you too drunk for that?"

Bryce shrugged, giving a cocky chuckle as he withdrew into the doorway. "The only way to get better at drunk driving is to practice."

Like any cop in this town would dare to give him a DUI. He'd been caught drinking and driving multiple times. As soon as those pigs read the name on his driver's license, they backed off real quick. Occasionally, one of them would deign to call Bryce's father, but the most Bryce got from him was a twenty-minute lecture.

On his drive home, Bryce kept the windows of his silver Cadillac Escalade EXT rolled down. The Savannah wind felt good on his flushed skin while heat from the tequila still warmed his body.

He was just the right amount of tipsy. Just enough to make his worries seem not so pressing.

The closer he drew to his house, the more the skyline in front of him became dotted with the sparkle of stars. His family farm encompassed hundreds of acres of land, far out of view of the city streetlights.

Bryce had his own home on his own plot of land. It had started out as a guest house, but he'd torn that old thing down and built himself a home he could be proud of. Adjoining his family's property, it was distanced from the main homestead, so his dad rarely saw the onslaught of women coming in and out of his place.

His mom? He didn't like to think about her. About how her body had been devoured by the cancer. Or how disappointed she would be to see him drinking himself into a stupor most nights.

"I'm going to do something good, Mom." He glanced out the window at the stars that seemed to twinkle in response. "You'll be proud of me. I promise."

In fact, he was going to start acting on that promise on Monday.

As he pulled up on the bumpy gravel road that led to his house, a familiar car was parked out front. Shit. Had he forgotten they were getting together? Bryce racked his mind but couldn't think of anything. He wasn't the kind to keep a strict schedule.

His Escalade pulled to a slow stop, and he left it running as he hopped out. The windows of her car were down as well, so Bryce hollered toward the car. "Hey, sweetheart, were we supposed to chill tonight?" He was damned glad he hadn't brought the skinny blonde home now. "I hope you weren't waiting long. I'm down to hang, though." In fact, he was already growing hard. Bryce lowered his head to look through the car window. "I just—"

He stopped when he realized he was talking to no one. The vehicle was empty, even though the headlights were on, illuminating the path in front of him.

He started to turn. "What the—?"

Something slammed against his temple.

The blow to his head didn't hurt. Not at first. It was too much of a shock for Bryce's body to process the pain. As he tried to stand, his feet crisscrossed and the world begin to spin harder, and not in the familiar way that binging on alcohol made the room turn. No, this was far more severe, bringing bile to his throat.

He fell to his knees as his vision narrowed, and a new source of bright hot pain went through his wrist just before his body hit the ground. Bryce held onto the last bit of consciousness as his cheek pressed into the stinging gravel.

The headlights faded…

When Bryce's eyes fluttered open again, he had no idea how much time had passed. Was the sun up? No, that wasn't the sun lighting up the barn. It was from a flashlight sitting just a few feet away.

Hay pushed through the thin material of his pants and scratched at Bryce's calves, forcing him to take in his surroundings despite his searing headache. Why the hell was he sitting on a bale of hay in one of the barns?

He reached down to relieve his now itchy legs, but his arm refused to move forward. He yanked at it, only to discover his hands were bound behind his back.

The memories of what happened flooded his senses. Someone had hit him in the head, but why? He didn't have time to figure it out. Adrenaline rushed in, and he managed to get to his feet before running toward the open barn doors.

Before he was halfway there, two figures appeared in the opening. Was it two people, or was Bryce seeing double? He was still intensely dizzy, having to force one foot in front of the other. He squinted. The headlights behind them turned their images into silhouettes, but it was definitely two people. One was her. The other was…wait, what was *he* doing here?

"What's going on, man? Why am I tied up? This some type of joke?"

They'd been friends for years. This made no sense. As his buddy approached, Bryce half-expected him to help with the restraints.

He got a sucker punch to the stomach instead.

"What the—?"

Bryce's voice was hoarse as he recoiled from the blow, stumbling backward. It took all his effort to stay on his feet.

He failed when the man in the ski mask delivered a second punch. Bryce doubled over in pain, causing him to gasp for a breath. The late steak dinner he'd eaten before heading to the bar was now threatening to come up. He used to think the term "seeing stars" was just an expression, but the twinkling he had witnessed while driving home had followed him into the barn. Little fireballs danced in his vision.

From their stalls, horses began to grow restless, some blowing in agitation.

Hands gripped the top of his arms, thrusting him backward. Bryce was too disoriented to do anything but go along with it. His fight left him...until a rough material scratched against Bryce's neck. He knew instantly what it was.

Growing up on a farm, you became well acquainted with the way thick rope felt against your skin. Not that he actually worked much, but he and his cousins used to try to wrangle each other like farm animals with any spare rope they found.

"No, no!" Bryce used every bit of energy he had to push his body forward, but it only made the rope tighter around his throat.

"Hurry up!" He heard someone yell, but Bryce's heart was beating in his ears so loudly, he couldn't tell who had spoken.

"Don't do this! You were right...I won't say a thing. I'm so sorry!" In his weakened state, hands bound behind him and, outnumbered, there was no fighting these guys. Bryce's last and only defense was to beg.

But his pleading did nothing to stop his feet from rising from the floor. He stumbled to his tiptoes, loose hay sliding along the hardwood against his foot. His airway was already constricted, and within seconds, only rough gasps traveled in and out of his mouth.

"Put your weight into it and fucking pull!"

The rope tightened, and he was thrust upward several

more inches, then several more. A ladder stood just a few feet from Bryce. *Not one of the brands his father normally bought for the farm. Why had the thought even crossed his mind?* The ladder, the rope...it all clicked for Bryce in his last moment. He knew exactly why his friend would do this.

Because of freaking animals.

But it was too late to do anything about it.

As he was pulled farther and farther into the air, the horses in the stalls became visible. Jennifer, his favorite, looked terrified, her eyes rolling as harsh breaths blew from her nostrils.

He focused on the animal as his vision dimmed and his lungs burned for air. She was such a good girl, strong but gentle. She didn't look gentle now.

The last thing he saw was Jennifer rear back, her front legs higher than the stall. It was almost like she was trying to escape, trying to save him.

Sorry, girl.

2

Detective Charlotte Cross stared at her boss, hoping she'd drifted to sleep at her desk and that Sergeant Ruth Morris wasn't standing in her office doorway.

She blinked, but her boss's figure remained where she stood. It was a Saturday, for goodness' sake, and Charli had only come into the office to finish up the paperwork on the evil bastard she'd just caught for killing several young girls.

"Can you please say that again?"

Ruth looked annoyed, the smooth dark skin of her face tightening into a frown. "I said that a young man was just found hanging inside his own stable."

That's what Charli thought she'd said, but she still couldn't figure out why Ruth was bringing this information to her. Suicides didn't fall under her division. As a detective with the Savannah Police Department, she investigated criminal cases. Though it certainly felt criminal when someone took their own life, those sad cases were not usually dropped onto her desk.

Charli let out a small sigh, hoping with all her heart that Ruth wasn't about to ask her to lead a press conference or something public relations related like that. Whenever her sergeant needed a favor, it usually involved dealing with the public in some manner. Whether it was a press conference or visiting a victim's family, the last thing Charli wanted to do was take time out of her day to interact with other people. It wasn't her strongest suit.

And Ruth knew it.

Charli sat back in her chair, mentally preparing herself for the worst. "What do you need me to do?"

"I need you to make a house call. I've got a man claiming foul play in his son's apparent suicide." Ruth rubbed her eyes. Her exhaustion was palpable.

Charli couldn't blame her. She was also exhausted after the crazy case they'd just had.

"A suicide? But why would I have to go out for a suicide? Forensics would have gone over this already, right? Do they have reason to expect foul play?"

"No, not really. They haven't finished with their investigation, so there is always the chance something else will pop up, but from the original scene, it looks to be a straightforward hanging. No immediate evidence of a struggle or signs that anyone else was present. We're still waiting for forensics to finish up at the site, though."

Charli raised her eyebrows, waiting for the explanation that must be forthcoming. It wasn't routine to send a detective out to an investigation after a suicide. Not even when a family insisted their loved one didn't kill themselves.

Sadly, it was fairly common for family members to refuse to believe someone had ended their own life. It created too much guilt. Suicides left lingering questions that had no easy answer. But to go out to a family and entertain the idea there may have been foul play only gave them false hope and hindered the grieving process.

Ruth closed the door behind her. "If I can be quite frank

with you, we're dealing with a pillar of the community. I'm sure you've heard of Mowery Homes."

Charli nearly said "duh" but managed to keep the sound behind her teeth. "Of course. I drive by two of their new housing development signs on my way to work."

"Montgomery Mowery runs that company as well as several substantial farms. His son was found hanging in one of their barns."

Charli wrinkled her nose. "I refuse to buy their eggs because they keep those poor chickens in cages all their lives."

Ruth gave Charli a stern look for interrupting before going on. "I'd love to live in a world where we treat the poorest of our citizens the same as the rich. Lord knows that would have benefited my family greatly growing up. And while I try to give fair attention to all our cases, the reality is that someone like Montgomery Mowery will usually receive special treatment. He's got a lot of ties to local politicians, and I don't need the department coming up in a negative light."

"Okay, fine, so we're playing the game a little." Charli could get behind this. "But why me?"

Ruth shook her head. She was clearly in no mood for Charli's griping, but what did she expect? Her boss knew Charli loathed these kinds of tasks. There were other detectives on the force who would complain a lot less about dealing with this. Besides, she'd been at the station late last night and then early again this morning. It was a Saturday, for goodness' sake. She could have just stayed in bed, but no...

"Your face has been plastered all over the news since you brought in the Marsh Killer. You're the city's hero. I have no doubt that Montgomery knows who you are, and I want him to know we're sending our very best."

Charli had to forcibly hold back an eye roll and glanced down at all the Marsh Killer paperwork she was still working on. It hadn't even been twenty-four hours since she arrested the man for killing teenage girls. Plus, it was a weekend, for cripes' sake.

"If I knew doing my job well was going to mean I had to placate a bunch of rich people, I would've stopped saving lives years ago."

"Hardy har." Ruth was scary when she was being sarcastic.

Charli held up a hand, wishing she had a white flag she could wave. "Okay, fine. I guess I'll head out there…all by myself…on a Saturday."

Her partner, Matthew Church, had hopped on a plane as soon as they'd closed their last case, heading to California to see his estranged daughter and ex-wife. The deaths of so many teen girls had gotten to Matthew more than Charli had even imagined. Almost as soon as the case was closed, he'd reported that he was going to visit Chelsea.

Ruth's expression turned lethal. "Since you're on salary… yes, you're going alone on a Saturday."

Charli held back a sigh. She didn't like working cases without Matthew.

As a rational, by-the-book detective, Charli didn't believe in gut feelings, instead relying on facts and figures to run her investigations. Matthew was the opposite, often letting instinct lead his work. He could be a bit of a hothead at times while Charli remained impartial.

Ruth had paired them together as partners, thinking their differences would complement each other. Nobody thought the pairing would last except the steely eyed sergeant. With her many years of experience, Charli had come to trust that her boss knew what she was doing. She'd been right. They'd become the most effective partnership at the precinct.

"Besides, he doesn't need to help you with this. It's a very simple task. One I know you can handle alone." Ruth's eyes narrowed, and Charli knew better than respond. "If it wasn't Montgomery Mowery who was asking, I wouldn't even be sending one detective. Daddy can bemoan all he wants, but it's probably a suicide."

There was no arguing this. As much as Charli wanted Matthew by her side, this really wasn't a two-person job. Not that his presence wouldn't help her. When she had these types of home visits to make, she always appreciated him.

Charli grabbed her ever-present notepad and pen. "Anything I need to know about the case?"

Ruth handed Charli a file. "Besides what you'll find in here, just be aware that Bryce Mowery was a troubled individual. He had constant run-ins with the law."

"He has a record?"

"Nope." This time, Ruth's scowl wasn't directed at Charli but at the slim folder in her hand. "A lot of incident reports made about him, but no arrests. No beat cop has any interest in taking on the Mowery family in court. Any arrest would have been challenged by the best lawyers money can buy. He got away with a lot, but it's clear something was wrong with him. Plenty of bar fights, drunk driving. He definitely had a substance abuse problem."

The more Charli heard, the more the signs did indeed point to suicide.

"Get out there as soon as possible." Ruth huffed again. "Nobody keeps Montgomery Mowery waiting."

3

The porcelain toilet seat was cool on my cheeks but did nothing for the rest of my languishing body. Every time I puked, waves of heat rolled through me. It'd been three times already. Surely there wasn't anything left in my gut to expel.

I slammed the toilet lid shut, reaching for the silver handle to flush away my shame. Guilt swirled down the bowl along with the contents of my stomach.

I never thought in a million years I could actually take a human life. Yeah, Bryce was a little bastard, and I didn't care that he was gone. Nobody liked him. Even his dad seemed indifferent to him after thirty years of bad decisions.

Still, I didn't believe I'd be the one to end him. There was something surreal about looking at myself in the mirror after watching his lifeless body swing from that barn roof beam. Kinda like that time I took mushrooms my senior year and tried to piece my own face together in the park bathroom. No matter how long I stared then, nothing quite came out right. It didn't look like me, even though I knew it was.

Now, my reflection showed a different man. There was

no going back after you took a life, no remembering a world before you snuffed out someone's child. The thought of the whole scene nauseated me. But it wasn't the light leaving Bryce's eyes that scared me the most.

If I was being completely honest with myself, a part of me enjoyed it. I didn't want to. I'd been terrified during the act, but watching Bryce writhe as he gasped his last breaths left me feeling…powerful.

Men like Bryce believed power was in money. They tossed their stacks of cash around as if it were nothing. They used what their fathers built to get everything they wanted in life.

But that was not true power, only cowardice. Bryce was a failure of a man, never doing anything for himself. Genuine power came when you designed it.

And that was what I'd done. I wasn't born into a family like Bryce. Riches weren't handed to me. Unlike him, I had to scratch and claw for everything I had.

And kill.

I hadn't puked when I'd killed the first man, but again, that asshole had been a stranger, not a friend. That must have been the difference. As much as Bryce needed to die, a part of me would always miss him.

My muscles screeched as I took a step. Small bruises had already established on my fists where I had punched Bryce. Blisters formed on my hands where I'd tightly gripped the rope that took Bryce's last breath.

I was still uneasy rising, both from the nausea and the workout I'd gotten hauling Bryce's unconscious body to the barn practically by myself. She'd tried to help but kept dropping his legs. Women. Good for nothing.

Well…except for one thing.

Having managed to stand, I steadied myself against the pedestal bathroom sink.

The white framed mirror above it revealed a splotchy face with weary eyes. Anxiety over what I'd just done permeated me. This face told a story I didn't want it to tell, that I didn't want anyone to know.

Squinting at myself, I smiled. If a small part of me was happy about killing Bryce, that was the part I'd show to the world.

4

Dust kicked up around Charli's tires, obstructing her view and forcing her to drive at a lower speed. She'd been instructed to meet Montgomery Mowery at the barn closest to Bryce's home, which was located on an adjoining property next to the Mowery estate.

She couldn't imagine living so close to her father as an adult. Charli loved him, but she butted heads enough with him as it was. Besides, she was too independent. She didn't like anyone telling her what to do.

"Call your dad."

Those were the last words Matthew said to her before he left to catch his flight. He'd looked so sincere when he'd said them that her heart squeezed at the memory.

He was right. She needed to call her dad.

But first, she needed to get face-to-face with another father and listen to the reasons his son wouldn't take his own life.

Dammit. She seriously hated this.

Charli eventually found her way when she recognized Randal Soames's vehicle parked outside a weathered barn.

18 MARY STONE & DONNA BERDEL

Wow.

The Mowerys really did have a long reach if they were able to get the Georgia Bureau of Investigation's medical examiner to a potential suicide scene.

The M.E. was standing in front of a six-foot tall man with salt-and-pepper hair, a sullen expression plastered on his face. That had to be Montgomery Mowery.

Charli stepped out of her car, her shoes kicking up a cloud of dirt. She raised a hand to block out the sun that hung high over the red barn with wood splintered at the sides. It was an old building, which seemed like a weird choice for a suicide attempt when his beautiful house sat only a hundred or so yards away. Why not choose to die within the comfort of his own home?

Since Soames was still engaging Mowery, Charli walked past them and into the barn, which was taped off for the scene. After signing into the crime log, she ducked under the neon yellow tape and realized why Bryce might have chosen this location. Along the roof were several solid almond-colored beams. They would make it easy to throw a rope around and have adequate height to hang oneself.

She'd need to check to see if his house had a rafter that would work as well. If it did, why would he have chosen this location instead?

And what had happened in his life to make him feel that ending it all was his best and only solution?

The stink of horse and their excrement filled her sinuses, but a peek into the stalls showed that all the animals were gone. Probably taken out to the pasture, but she made a note to double-check.

She was surprised to find that the body was already gone, taken by Soames's team. Had Mowery contacted the GBI first? The idea grated but wasn't a surprise. Charli wouldn't have been shocked to find the FBI landing a helicopter in a nearby field. Money made people jump.

Speaking of jumping...

Looking up, she noted that the noose still hung high. One forensic photographer was taking photos while another tech measured the height. A tall ladder was on its side, and she tried to put herself in Bryce's shoes. What had it taken to walk to this barn, set up a ladder, and toss a rope over the beam? Tie a knot and put it around his neck?

Poor kid.

Had he been filled with regret the moment he'd kicked the ladder to the side, or had he simply waited for the pain that must have been overwhelming him to fade away?

Despite Bryce's reputation, Charli's heart broke a little. Most people had it in their heads that death by hanging was a quick and efficient way to go, but it often wasn't. Unless you fell in the exact right position, which many didn't, you suffocated slowly over the course of several minutes. Bryce likely didn't know what a slow, agonizing demise he was choosing for himself. Nobody deserved that.

Charli made her way back outside. Soames was eyeing her as she approached him and the dead man's father.

"Montgomery Mowery, I'm Detective Cross." Charli nodded, hoping he wouldn't extend his hand. She wasn't one of those touchy-feely people, especially with people she didn't know. Who knew where his hand had last been?

Picking his nose? Wiping his butt? Wanking off?

Charli swallowed down the surge of bile that threatened to embarrass her and put on her very best sympathetic face. This man, wealth or no wealth, had just lost a child. She didn't need to be worrying about his hand or any other body parts.

"Detective Cross, yes, I recognize you." He thankfully kept

his hands by his sides. "Very good work you did with catching that twisted serial killer. I'm hoping you can do similar work with helping me find out who murdered my boy."

His voice was definitive. There was no question in Montgomery Mowery's mind that this was not a suicide.

"I certainly want to help you get to the bottom of this." Charli pulled out her notebook. "First, I want to obtain information from Dr. Soames. He worked closely with me on our last investigation."

Soames gave a soft but somber smile. While the world was celebrating what they'd done, it was still unpleasant for them both to remember some of the brutality from their last case. A suicide was a cakewalk by comparison to all those teen girls who'd been brutalized in their final moments.

"We're waiting on specifics from the lab, but based on the state of rigor mortis, I'd say his death occurred between eight and sixteen hours ago. The subject had definitely been drinking beforehand. Initial findings are consistent with a suicide by hanging."

"If you're as good as Detective Cross claims you are, you'll find out fast that isn't the case." Montgomery Mowery swallowed hard, as if trying to hold back from saying anything more aggressive.

Dr. Randal Soames, who usually didn't clam up around anyone, held his tongue. Apparently, he too understood the importance of keeping Montgomery Mowery happy.

Charli diverted her attention to the grieving father. "What can you tell me about what happened? Were you the one who found the body?"

"I was. He was supposed to meet me for a late breakfast this morning, and when he didn't show or answer his phone, I have to admit that I came storming over to find him. I hadn't heard from Bryce in two days, and I assumed he had taken one of his unannounced trips to either L.A. or New

Orleans. He likes..." The man swallowed hard, his face twisting with the emotion he tried to hold back. "He *liked* to run off about once a month. Get drunk, spend a lot of money at strip clubs, that kind of thing."

Even through the pain, Charli couldn't help but note the contempt in Montgomery's voice. "You sound upset about that."

Mowery shifted his weight on one leg, the defensiveness rolling off him in waves. "Well, yeah, I didn't like that my boy was so reckless. I tried to teach him the value of a hard-earned dollar. When I was his age, I was already running my own million-dollar company from the ground up. Sometimes, I felt I failed him as a father that he could live his life with such carelessness." He coughed into his hand. "I'm feeling that even harder now."

Despite his anger about his son's lifestyle, underneath the frustration was a hurting father. Sadness and anger were closely related emotions, especially in incidents of suicide. There was an overwhelming feeling of loss and resentment that a loved one could leave this Earth knowing the pain that would follow. Guilt for believing they could have done something to prevent it.

"I'm sorry, I know how difficult this must be for you." With the anguish that danced in Mowery's eyes, Charli didn't relish pushing him into rehashing the details of how Bryce was found.

Thankfully, she didn't have to. Montgomery Mowery straightened and continued. "Anyway, I was expecting to come out here and find him missing, but I saw his Escalade parked in his driveway, so I knew he was home. He always parks it at the airport when he leaves. He hated calling for a cab. So, I storm into the house, thinking I'd see him laid up with some pretty young thing, sleeping off a hangover. But he was nowhere to be found."

Charli took meticulous notes, glancing up at Mowery between bullet points. "And what did you do when you couldn't find him?"

"Well, on the way back to my car, I called his phone again and heard it ringing in the Escalade. That worried me a little, but not too much because, when Bryce is drunk, he leaves his phone in stupid places. He's lost it on more than one occasion. Then I started thinking he might have taken a young lady to ride one of the horses. He does that sometimes. I don't know why, part of his seduction plan or something."

Bryce was a womanizer, it seemed. At least in the eyes of his father. Charli didn't want to write those exact words down and instead opted for "enjoys late-night dalliances with various women." That was eloquent enough that even if Montgomery Mowery were reading over her shoulder, he couldn't get too upset.

She made eye contact with him once again. "Did you go home after you decided he must be out riding?"

"No, because I know how risky it can be to ride a horse drunk. Not as dangerous as drunk driving, mind you, but still perilous. Horses like to be ridden by a stable-minded person, someone they can trust. Alcohol throws off that trust, so I wanted to know which horse he'd taken out. If he rode Jennifer, I knew he was probably all right. That's his horse. I made my way into the stables and then I saw him."

Mowery's chin quivered. He did his best to keep his expression hard. He was an old-school man of the South, and Charli suspected that he didn't want to reveal his emotions. They betrayed him anyway.

"I'm very sorry for your loss." Though she didn't like to touch people, she couldn't stop herself from reaching out and squeezing his arm. "I know how difficult it can be to accept that your son made such a drastic choice to end his life."

Montgomery's brow tightened, and he shook her hand

off. "Bryce absolutely did not kill himself. He wouldn't do that."

Charli waited until he met her gaze. "With all due respect, why are you so adamant that your son wouldn't hurt himself? Do you know anybody who wished him harm?"

"No, I don't, but I know how much my son loved his life. He wasn't a hard worker, sure, but that's because he had it made. He had all the money he could want. He had girls hanging off him. He had respect in this town. The kid vacationed monthly. He did whatever he pleased. You expect me to believe that a man who had everything he could ever want would toss it all aside?"

Soames shifted on the gravel. "Sometimes, it's the people with everything who are hiding their inner world the most."

"No, not my boy." Mowery looked hard at the M.E. "I know who he is. This isn't something he'd do."

Soames wasn't wrong. People could often appear to have idyllic lives and still be deeply depressed. But Charli was inclined to agree with Mowery. Bryce didn't seem to fit the profile of a secretly wounded man. Most rich and entitled men were too narcissistic to take themselves out of the world.

Charli tucked her notepad into her pocket. "Mind if I look around the house?"

"Your guys have already been through there, but be my guest."

Charli wondered who he meant by "your guys" but kept the question to herself. She'd puzzle all those pieces together later.

Deciding to walk the short distance, she gave a slow whistle as she approached Bryce Mowery's home. It looked a little out of place on such a wide-open piece of farmland. *Extravagant* and *ornate* were the first words that came to mind, but to her, it would have been better suited on the beach.

Despite being extravagant on the outside, the ornate home was a disaster once she walked through the front doors. All over the house were random wrappers and empty bottles of alcohol. Bryce probably grew up with maids his entire life and had no idea how to clean up after himself. Typical.

Charli gave herself a mental check. She hated when her humanness came out, overriding her desire to be objective. Just because the man was rich didn't mean he was bad or wrong, and she needed to quit focusing on his wealth and focus on what happened in the last eight to sixteen hours or so that cost him his life, by his own hand or otherwise.

"What happened to you, Bryce Mowery?" Her low voice seemed to echo through the cavernous living room.

Mess in itself was no indicator of murder. As Charli moved through the rooms, nothing about its haphazard style suggested anyone had been here except the owner.

Until she got to the bedroom. Bryce's room was no cleaner than the rest of his house. Red silk bedsheets were crumpled on top of the bed, half fallen to the floor. An empty condom wrapper sat on one of the cherrywood bedside tables.

Charli stepped around to get a view of the other table where a lamp was still on, which seemed a little bizarre. Had the man woken, turned the light on, and decided to end his life?

Must have been one heck of a nightmare if that was the case.

Next to the bedside table was a watch. By the looks of it, a very expensive one. It was facedown, as if it had been knocked over. Charli used her phone to take a picture of its position before making a note to have the crime scene team check it out.

Maybe it was nothing, but the watch stood out to Charli. Yes, Bryce was messy, but throughout the house, none of the trash on the tables or floors had been valuable. Bryce clearly enjoyed high-end items and appeared to take care of them. Was he the type to let an expensive watch fall on the floor and not pick it up?

Maybe. Or maybe not.

It was enough to open Charli up to the possibility that someone else might have been present in the house. She scoured the residence for anything else out of the ordinary but found nothing.

On her way back to the road, she glued her eyes to the ground, as she often did when she was analyzing a case. It was easier to fixate on one point than to let her eyes drift around. Was there anything else she'd seen in the barn that could have been a clue? She knew Soames would have the forensic techs dust the barn door and ladder Bryce would've stood on for prints. Or they could—

Something went askew in her sightline. It was subtle, and for a moment, she doubted she was seeing anything at all. But as she studied the area, it became more obvious. The gravel next to her feet had shifted. One layer of pebbles was higher than the other, leaving a sort of trail.

She followed the trail to where it stopped. The gravel was relatively smooth for ten or so feet before the lines started again.

Drag marks?

Possibly. Or they could have been from a wheelbarrow or some other type of thin wheeled vehicle. But why start and stop like this if that were the case?

Crouching down, she took additional pictures and made a note to ask one of the crime scene techs to make sure they photographed this area too. They needed to check the heels of Bryce's boots as well, to see if they had marks that would indicate he'd been dragged.

If Bryce Mowery was truly a victim of a crime, she'd need every single piece of evidence she could gather to prove he hadn't harmed himself.

As she followed the trail, she bit her lip. Someone had definitely dragged something heavy along this path, but what?

She'd do her darndest to find out.

5

Charli sat at her desk at the precinct, going over the last of the details she'd pried from Montgomery Mowery before leaving. There wasn't much to go on. Bryce apparently didn't have many friends he was in close contact with. According to Montgomery, "Bryce was very selective with who he allowed into his life on a personal level. Being so wealthy makes one leery that people only want to get close to get something from you."

Except bed buddies. Bryce didn't appear to be very selective about who he got personal with between the sheets.

Montgomery Mowery did give her a couple of names. One was Roland Lierman, a buddy from high school Bryce spent a fair amount of time with. To her surprise, Mowery apparently had a girlfriend, despite Bryce's antics with women. Blair Daughtry. Mowery had practically sneered the woman's name, stating that she would often go barhopping with his son at some of the bougie spots downtown.

After pressing the silver power button on her desktop tower, Charli sat back and waited. The ancient computer always took forever to turn on. Charli didn't normally mind.

She'd use this time to swerve around in her desk chair and bother Matthew about whatever he was doing.

The office was hollow without him.

Since it was a Saturday, the detective bullpen was pretty empty too. Not even Janice Piper was there, not that Charli terribly missed her presence. There was Ruth, but she'd been holed up in her office on the phone with the mayor when Charli arrived back at the precinct.

She'd caught just a few sentences from the conversation coming out loud and clear on the sergeant's speakerphone, and it was obvious to Charli the mayor was asking about Bryce Mowery and wanted Ruth to make sure to plug any holes so the media wasn't alerted. How important did someone have to be that the freaking mayor called on their behalf?

Mowery's final words played back through her mind. *"No press, you hear me? Not until you've nailed the bastard who did this to my son."*

At the time, Charli thought it had been wishful thinking, but after hearing the mayor's conversation with her boss, she wasn't so sure. Not that she minded not having the press shouting out a million stupid questions. The media had their advantages, but those good points were often overshadowed by their desire to be the first to air a story. In those cases, they could be brutal.

As soon as the computer ground to life, she opened social media channels for the local press stations. She sighed in relief. Nothing about Bryce Mowery's death…yet.

Charli's stomach turned as she thought about when they inevitably would. She'd experienced enough of the press for a lifetime. Not that she'd ever admit it out loud, but a small part of her selfishly hoped Bryce had indeed killed himself so she could avoid the limelight entirely. Charli didn't need another high-profile case, especially not so soon after the last one.

Still, Charli vowed to be thorough, and there were a few discrepancies in the case. Montgomery Mowery wasn't wrong. Bryce was living on easy street, so his suicide made little sense. And what was with that drag line in the gravel? It was a farm, so it could have been something benign. Regardless, Charli had emailed the crime scene team, asking them to send her the photos.

The first person she tried to look up was Blair Daughtry. If there was foul play involved in this case, it was best to consider the victim's romantic interests. Bryce's insatiable desire for other women could definitely turn a scorned lover to violence.

There wasn't much to find on Blair, though. She had no criminal record. Charli was able to pull up a few social media profiles, but the girl was smart enough to keep everything private. The only thing viewable was her photo. She had maroon hair, not the kind of red one was born with. She absolutely got that color from a bottle, but it actually shined nicely against her bright green eyes. Charli wasn't usually one for unnatural hair colors, but it was a good look on her.

Charli's finger rapped softly against her scratched desk. Years of scribbling notes had done its damage on the top. Little etchings of past words were sketched in the surface. While the chaos of all the lines might bother someone else, for Charli, they were evidence this office was home.

She shifted her fingers from the desktop back to her warm keyboard to look up Roland Lierman. Unlike Blair, Roland actually had several priors. One was public drunkenness, the other marijuana distribution. If rumor was true, these were the same types of crimes that Bryce himself had engaged in at some point, but Roland apparently didn't have the kind of parents who could get a kid out of petty crime charges.

She wrote his address down in her notebook in blue ink, circling it so it would be easy to find in her many pages of notes. Even on a case as small as this, Charli made sure she was flush with relevant details.

Right above Roland's address was another fact that caught her eye. Montgomery had mentioned how Bryce, who once frequented sleazy strip clubs near the Savannah area, had since advanced to high-end bars. Evidently, this was his most frequent activity.

As far as Charli knew, Roland hadn't been with Bryce on his final night, but his father did believe he was at a bar. She should prioritize going to whatever location he'd been seen in last, so she could interview people while the details were still fresh in their minds.

But where to start? She made a note to file for a warrant to obtain Bryce's credit card statements.

Charli wasn't familiar with the many bars downtown. She didn't make it a habit to go out drinking, as Matthew liked to do, and she'd never be caught dead at a bar that overcharged for a basic cocktail. She didn't earn enough to frequent the businesses downtown. They catered to a very specific demographic.

But it was a demographic that Tim McBride met. She was pretty sure she'd seen him on her way in. Unlike most of the guys on duty, Tim wasn't from a working-class background. His family owned several grocery stores in Savannah and threw an extravagant charity ball every year. Office gossip said that his family wasn't too happy with him for foregoing the grocery business to be a cop.

Charli lucked out and found him at his desk, sipping a coffee as he joked with a few other on-duty officers.

"McBride, I need to pick your brain." Charli didn't bother

asking permission to question him. She'd learned early in her career if she didn't speak from a place of authority, she wouldn't command respect.

It wasn't just that she was a woman, although that certainly played a part. It also had a lot to do with her physicality. She was short, baby-faced, her pixie cut framing her apple cheeks. Everything about Charli screamed cute, and it was only in her voice and posture that she could fight this image.

"What do you need to know?" McBride set his coffee down on his desk, giving her his full attention.

"If I wanted to go to the fanciest bar downtown, where should I head?"

There was a murmur from behind Charli's back. "What, you got a hot date to get to?"

Charli could whip around and confront the snide remark but decided against it. The last few days had taken a lot out of her. While she might normally address the obnoxious sexism some of the lower-ranking cops still threw at her, she didn't have the energy today.

"I mean, I guess it depends on the atmosphere you're looking for. But if you're going on reputation alone, probably Olive's Lounge." Tim McBride was classy enough to pretend he hadn't heard the rude comment.

"Olive's Lounge, huh? Would you call that the most expensive place to get a drink?"

"Oh, absolutely. Nowhere better to waste a buck than Olive's."

Then that was where Charli would head first.

6

Charli stood outside of her car for a minute, letting the AC kick on before sitting on the sweltering front seat. Not that standing in the sun was much of an improvement. It was a sauna inside the car and a steam room outside. Typical humid September day in Georgia. At least there was just a month and a half or so until the leaves began to change.

Leaning against the car window, she resisted the urge to call Matthew. She only wanted to catch him up on what she was doing, but she didn't want to interfere with his much-needed time with his daughter.

Oh, what the hell? Charli couldn't take it anymore.

There was an empty space in both her car and office without Matthew by her side. Although normally solitude was refreshing for her, even someone as introverted as Charli needed some kind of human contact.

And Matthew was far more than her partner. He was a friend. Not just a friend, but a best friend, the only person she'd been close to—except for her mother before she passed —since Madeline's death. It wasn't easy to let people in, not after what had happened.

She stepped into her car. The air wasn't quite cold yet, but cool enough to be bearable. Slamming the door behind her, she dialed Matthew's number, and the phone rang over her speakers.

"Hey, Smalls."

She grinned, even though she hated the nickname. "Hey, Bigs. How's it going?"

He groaned, and her smile faded. That didn't sound good. "It's going exactly nowhere, if the truth be told."

Her heart cracked a little at his words. "I'm sorry. Have you seen Chelsea?"

Matthew was silent for a very long time. "For about five minutes this morning. She's apparently spending the weekend with a couple girlfriends and going to some K-pop concert tonight." He sighed so hard that the air created static over the line.

"So, you won't be able to see her at all?"

"Nope." There was so much sadness in the word that Charli's heart ached.

"Have you seen Judy?"

Another long groan. "Unfortunately...and her new fella."

Oh boy.

After the divorce, Judy had moved to California with the man she'd fallen in love with while married to Matthew. That hadn't lasted, of course, but it seemed a new man had slid right in to take the other one's place.

Charli wasn't sure what to say to that, so instead of keeping her mouth closed, she changed the subject. "I'm working this case and—"

"You are?" Matthew cut her off, an edge to his voice. "Alone?"

"Well, it's not even really a case. Ruth has sent me on a wild goose chase because some rich kid killed himself and his dad is demanding we investigate further. There's not much for me to do, but Ruth seems stressed about it, so I'm trying to be thorough."

Matthew let out a small sigh of relief. "Got it. So, while I'm twiddling my thumbs here, you get to play lackey for Savannah's elite?"

"Pretty much, yeah. Was wondering if you knew anything about them that I didn't, actually. The son is Bryce Mowery. Father is Montgomery Mowery."

He whistled loud and long. "The Mowery family? Of course I know them. Who the hell doesn't?"

"Me, apparently. I mean, I know who they are, but I've got no clue about their personal lives."

Matthew's voice picked up, as it always did when he was gossiping. "Montgomery Mowery is a big time mogul. His development business alone is worth a good thirty million, and that doesn't include the farm business. Wife died a couple years ago of cancer, and I don't remember hearing any rumors about him remarrying or even having a girl-friend." He snorted. "Not that I run in those same social circles anyway."

That pretty much aligned with what Charli had learned so far. "And his son?"

"Bryce is a male version of a Kardashian. Rich and well-known for no other reason than the fact he's Montgomery's son. But everyone knows that kid is a grade A loser. Just another hard-drinking Richie Rich. Wait..." There was a short pause as Matthew finally pieced all the information together. "Are you telling me that Bryce killed himself?"

"He was found hanging in the horse stables this morning, I'm afraid. How do you know so much about him?"

"I came into contact with him quite a few times before becoming a detective. He drove through multiple DUI checkpoints completely hammered. I always wanted to throw the book at him, but the older cops on-site refused to do their damn job. Everyone is terrified of Montgomery. But I gotta say, something doesn't sit right with the idea that Bryce killed himself."

Charli wasn't surprised that Matthew already had a gut instinct leading his thought process. It was one annoying thing about working with the man. Sometimes, his gut was on the money, and other times, it gave him tunnel vision, or worse, kept him from seeing the facts of a case.

"I went out there a couple hours ago, and while I can't definitively say he didn't kill himself, I'm certainly open to that possibility. There were just a few details that stood out to me. An expensive watch left on the floor, drag patterns in the gravel in front of his house." Charli was coming up to a red light. As her car slowed to a stop, television noises from Matthew's hotel room became more evident. "Also, one of the techs called me a little bit ago to let me know that Bryce's vehicle was completely out of gas. It was like he'd left it running all night long."

"That's interesting. Maybe he was drunk and forgot to turn it off."

Charli considered the possibility. "Maybe. Or maybe he never made it into his house. If he was truly murdered, he could have been attacked outside his vehicle."

"How far is it from his vehicle to the barn?"

"Hundred yards or so, I'm guessing."

Matthew snorted. "What meathead would kill him at his car, then drag him all the way to that barn?"

Yeah…that was a good point.

"Maybe whoever did this didn't want to drive Bryce's vehicle in case they left hair or DNA?" It was only a guess but plausible.

Charli expected Matthew to shoot a hole in the theory, and he didn't disappoint. "The killer must have had a vehicle too. Why not use their own?"

She gave the question some thought. "Maybe for the same reason they didn't use Bryce's Escalade. They might have worried that Bryce would leave blood or some form of DNA or print in their vehicle. They could have just been overly cautious." She sighed. "Or, he might have just come home and decided to end it all."

"I'm telling you, Charli, that kid would never kill himself. I have never met a man more self-obsessed. In fact, you might wanna call up NASA and make sure that Earth is actually revolving around the sun and not Bryce Mowery's ego."

"That bad, huh?"

"The boy was an entitled punk. I heard Montgomery had high hopes that one day Bryce would take over the family business, but I can't see how Bryce would ever willfully choose to work. He partied, he vacationed, and he bossed around anyone he could. You definitely need to exhaust every other possible alternative to suicide."

Charli let out a small humming noise.

"What?" Matthew's voice was more like a growl.

"Nothing, but seems like you're pretty interested in my lame lackey case now, huh?" Charli teased.

"Oh, no, absolutely not. You have fun investigating the tangled web that is the Mowery family. I'll be here drinking a cold one, enjoying *Game of Thrones* while ordering room service. You ever watch this show, by the way? I think they just killed this Jon kid."

"You should probably exhaust all possible alternatives to that too." Charli smiled to herself.

"Huh?"

"Never mind, never mind." A thought occurred to her. "I can't remember if I told you, but Montgomery Mowery swears the ladder that was used when Bryce was killed is a brand he's never bought. Apparently, he's had some type of discount with one specific vendor for all equipment like that."

"Want me to work on finding who might have bought that ladder?"

Charli smiled, relieved not to have to call a hundred hardware stores herself. "Do you mind?"

"Nope. *Game of Thrones* will never be the same without Jon, so it'll give me something else to do."

"Thanks. I'll email you all the information in a little bit, but right now, I've got to go. I'm at Olive's Lounge. I'm going to see when Bryce was last here."

"Best of luck."

Charli pulled into an empty parking space in the back of the lot. There were quite a few other cars present. Clearly, this was a popular spot, even on a Saturday afternoon.

When Charli moved inside, she found a tall, dark-haired bartender busily shaking drinks. Her lips were plastered with a bright red lipstick that contrasted with her black uniform.

The bar was laid out with high-backed stools seated with several people, but the edge of the bar where a door opened on the counter for the staff to lift and walk through remained unblocked. Charli walked up to it, leaning against the dark granite. She waited patiently to be noticed by the bartender.

Some cops were aggressive about their time, stopping someone during any activity to demand an interview. Charli didn't believe that approach was helpful. Being inconsiderate of someone's schedule would not lead to them opening up about a case. And even aside from interview tactics, she had empathy for the working-class employees who had to cater to the rich assholes of Savannah. This woman's job was hard enough already if she had to serve people like Bryce.

It only took a minute for the bartender to notice her and mosey on over. "Can I help you?"

"Possibly. I'm Detective Cross." She showed the woman her shield. "I was hoping you could answer a few questions for me regarding a case I'm investigating."

Her eyes widened. "I don't know what I could help with, but sure."

Charli snapped open her field notepad. "What's your name?"

"Katie Willhelm."

Charli jotted the name down. "Did you happen to be working here last night?"

"Yep. From four to close, which is midnight."

"Are you familiar with Bryce Mowery?"

Katie ran a white rag over a heavy whiskey glass, her nose wrinkling for just a moment. "Oh, yeah, I know Bryce. He's a real pain in the ass."

The Mowerys had apparently managed to keep Bryce's suicide under wraps for now. At least, word hadn't gotten around the bar yet, and Charli wouldn't be the one to reveal such private information, especially not when it could piss off Montgomery Mowery and make life harder for Ruth.

"Was he in here last night?"

"Why?" Katie rolled her eyes. "What's he done now?"

"I'm sorry, but I can't discuss an ongoing investigation. Do you know if he was here last night?"

"Sure was. He ordered a bunch of shots and flirted with a girl across the bar. I used to work at a cafe down the street with his girlfriend, so I confronted him. He wanted to pay for the girl's drinks, and I pointed out he was dating someone. To which he replied it was none of my business, he was a Mowery, so buzz off. The guy is a total dick."

The guy sure sounded like one. "What's the person's name he was dating?"

"Blair Daughtry."

Charli recognized the name immediately. "Are you saying

that, although he was dating Blair Daughtry, he was planning to go home with this other girl?"

"Sure seemed like it. I don't think it happened. Don't know why. But he was definitely interested initially. At least enough to pick up her tab."

If Bryce had planned to kill himself, why would he be considering hooking up with some random girl at the bar? Again, there was always the chance the suicide was an impulsive move, one that Bryce didn't plan in advance.

"What was his mood like?"

Katie snorted. "Is arrogant a mood? I don't know, he looked like he usually did. He was having a good time. Flirting with women. He asked about Markus, the normal weekend bartender, and seemed a little pissed that he wasn't here because he was sick. He didn't joke with me or anything. I just moved from hosting to bartending a week or so ago. I don't think he even recognized me as regular staff."

"You don't think he seemed stressed or upset in any way?"

The bartender laughed out loud. "Are you kidding? No, I don't think Bryce knows the definition of stress."

The deeper she looked into Bryce's death, the more it didn't seem to add up. Matthew appeared to be right. Nobody thought Bryce was the type to end his own life.

The bartender leaned forward, her gaze fastened on Charli's face. "Please, tell me Bryce has gotten into trouble. Did he finally get arrested for drunk driving?"

Charli waved a hand. "He definitely got into some kind of trouble. Thank you for talking with me." She slid her card across the bar. "If you think of anything, please give me a call."

Katie pocketed the card. "Can I get you something to drink?"

It had been a long while since Charli had gone out. Though she told herself earlier she'd never pay for an overpriced cocktail at a place like this, once she looked around, she understood the allure.

She couldn't remember the last time she'd been somewhere this nice. Along the walls were emerald and gold art deco wallpaper. A dark wood crown molding lined the ceiling, which matched the wood of the bar front, shelves, and all the tables. It was positively elegant. Charli felt like she'd walked into a scene in *The Great Gatsby*.

"You know what? Sure, I'll take a virgin Midori sour."

What could one drink hurt, especially since it was nonalcoholic? Didn't she deserve a little treat? She was starting to wish she'd dressed up for the occasion. This wouldn't be a bad place to go on a date.

Inwardly, Charli cringed at the thought. What was this bougie bar doing to her? She hadn't considered dating in forever.

Of course, her dad was constantly reminding her she was getting older, that the clock was ticking. She didn't much care about his criticisms, but there was a small part of her that was starting to feel a void in her life, with loneliness hanging over her each night.

Perhaps it was because of her most recent investigation, which had placed her very best friend in the world at the forefront of her mind. Poor Madeline.

The dam holding her past in check burst, and a memory crashed over her, sweeping her back into the worst day of her life.

"I can't believe Mr. Ferris gave us a pop quiz in Bio today, ugh. It's like he knew I didn't do the reading last night." Madeline scratched her shoe in the dirt before glancing up at Charli with her mischievous grin. "Although I don't do the reading most nights, so I suppose his odds of catching me off guard were good."

Charli laughed. "Yet somehow, you probably managed to get an A anyway."

Madeline nudged Charli's ankle with her sneaker. "And so did you."

Sure, but that was because Charli studied. The idea of showing up unprepared for class made her stomach queasy. Madeline was the free-spirited one. She liked to wing things, and somehow, they always turned out. She made straight A's, was on student council, and was a star on the cross-country team. Life came easy for her, with her outgoing, bubbly personality and carefree nature.

Not so much for Charli. If the Myers-Briggs personality test that her psychology teacher had them take was legit, then she was the ISTJ to Madeline's ENFP.

The fact that Charli thought the Myers-Briggs was a bunch of made-up nonsense while Madeline read her horoscope every day said pretty much everything about the differences in their personalities a person might need to know about them.

They were complete opposites, yet together, they worked.

For instance, Charli would personally never hang around in the Bonaventure Cemetery, hoping some boy would decide to grace her with his presence. Not that she needed to worry about that happening since most of the boys in her classes thought she was bitchy.

She couldn't help it if she refused to coddle them and pretend like their obnoxious jokes were funny when they weren't or allow obviously wrong statements to go unchallenged. Their delicate egos were their problem, not hers.

For Madeline, though, Charli'd wait around for a boy in a graveyard beneath the Spanish moss because that's what she and Madeline did. They had each other's backs, no matter what.

Time passed as they chatted about anything and everything until Madeline finally checked her phone and sighed. "Okay, it's been half an hour now. Doesn't look like he's going to make it."

That cemented it. Teen boys were idiots because no one with a functional brain would pass up an invitation from Madeline. "Don't worry. He'll regret not coming. They always do."

The appreciative smile that lit up Madeline's face only made Charli more certain this boy was a dope.

Like she did on every occasion when they strolled through the cemetery after school, Madeline patted the statue of Savannah's fastest female marathoner three times before spinning away. Good luck, she claimed, for her cross-country meets.

Charli didn't believe in luck. She did, however, believe in Madeline.

As they left the weathered bronze likeness behind, Charli wondered, not for the first time, why Madeline had chosen her, of all people. She could have been best friends with anyone at school, but she'd picked Charli. An oddly outspoken girl who seemed like she was on a different wavelength than everyone else.

Charli shuddered to imagine how lonely her high school experience might have been had they not been seated next to each other in fifth grade.

Lucky for her, she never had to find out.

Madeline bounced along in her upbeat way, gushing in her superlative-laden manner about a new, ridiculously corny song she'd heard the night before. Charli was laughing so hard at her commentary that she stumbled over a dip in the path. The trip made her spot the white shoelace trailing in the dirt. Yuck. She hated that.

She bent down to tie the lace, noticed a knot, and began working it out while Madeline skipped ahead. As Charli picked away, a muffled squeak reached her ears, then a couple of grunts. A scraping sound followed, like shoes dragging in the dirt.

Charli snorted but didn't glance up. She was sooo close to loosening the stupid knot. "What the heck are you doing over there, choreographing a new dance?" Madeline was the only person Charli knew who'd sing and dance her way through a graveyard without batting an eye. Not a bashful bone in that girl's body.

With one more pull, the laces came free. "Yes! Finally!" She was tying them into a double knot when Madeline screamed.

That didn't sound like singing.

"Madeline?" Her head whipped up, and her heart skidded to a halt. Ahead, right by the wrought iron fence, a man was dragging a struggling Madeline backward toward the street.

"Stop!" As Charli sprang to her feet, her frantic gaze caught on the gray vehicle parked on the street behind them. Her stomach free-fell when the detail clicked.

A van. This strange man was taking Madeline to his van.

No! "Stop, let her go! Madeline!" Charli launched into a sprint, pumping her legs with all her strength. She had to catch them. She had to.

Two strides in, she recognized the truth, but she refused to accept it. She pushed herself harder, even as the intrusive voice repeated the same words with every step.

Too late. Too late. Too. Late.

She was still a good ten yards from the gate when the man stuffed Madeline into the large gray van with no windows and pealed out.

"Stop!" Charli ran screaming after them, a new litany pounding through her head.

This wasn't happening. This wasn't happening.

By the time she flew through the gate, tears streamed down her face. She kept running, though, spinning to the right and yanking her phone out to snap a photo. A license plate! If she got a picture of that, the police could find Madeline.

She pointed the camera at the van's rear bumper and held her finger on the button.

Tap tap tap tap tap! The shutter burst to life, snapping shot after shot in rapid succession. It took another second before Charli comprehended what she was seeing. Or more accurately, what she wasn't seeing.

When she did, she felt like her entire world had been turned inside out. Like the universe had stopped making any kind of sense.

The police wouldn't be able to track them down by using the license plate because the van didn't have one.

Their best chance of finding Madeline was gone.

"Here you go."

Charli snapped from the past and gazed at the green drink the bartender sat in front of her.

"Thank you." She reached for the glass with hands that trembled a little.

She used to have so much fun with Madeline, but now...

With her mom having passed, her strained relationship with her dad, and the lack of friends, it wasn't like that for her anymore. She used to be surrounded by loved ones daily, but now she only had her work colleagues. Maybe having someone to come home to would fill a void that had been building for a while.

And if looking for a man was the goal, this was the place to do it. With her drink in hand, she swirled in her chair to get a look at her prospects. She knew she wouldn't actually date anyone in here, but it was fun to fantasize for a moment.

"Charli, is that you?"

Charli's head was pulled to the right, and it took a minute to recognize the woman who'd approached.

"Rebecca? Rebecca Larson?"

"Yeah! Wow, I don't think I've seen you since high school." Rebecca came up and gave Charli a tight squeeze around the shoulders.

And Charli allowed it. In fact, she hugged Rebecca back. Hard.

They'd been friends in high school. Not as close as Charli and Madeline, of course, but Rebecca had hung out with both girls sometimes.

Guilt made Charli give Rebecca one last squeeze before letting her go. She'd often regretted allowing her grief to push everyone away after Madeline died. If she was lonely now, she had no one to blame but herself.

"What are you up to?" Rebecca's hazel eyes glistened under the lights. "I hear you're a detective now?"

"Sure am. That's actually what brings me here tonight. I've been asking around about Bryce Mowery."

"Uh oh, what did he do?" Rebecca sighed and tossed back her strawberry blonde hair. It was just as long as it'd been in high school, nearly down to her waist.

"You're familiar with him."

Rebecca shifted on her feet awkwardly, a glass of wine in hand. "Can I sit?"

"Yes, of course." Charli patted the stool next to her.

"Well," Rebecca lowered her voice, "between you and me, Bryce and I hooked up a few months ago."

Charli suppressed a smile. "You're kidding?"

Rebecca slapped a hand over her face. "I wish I was. It was nothing serious. Can't say I care for the guy, but I'd just broken up with my long-term boyfriend and I was feeling really insecure. I got too drunk and went home with him. Turns out, he actually has a girlfriend, so I noped out of that situation damn quick. It's embarrassing, so please don't tell anyone."

"I promise, your secret is safe with me." Charli meant it.

Sitting here now with Rebecca, nostalgia washed over her. Funny, she was just thinking about how she had no friends, and then Rebecca popped up. It was probably the universe's way of telling her the solution to her loneliness wasn't a man, but friendship.

"I'm surprised he isn't here right now, actually." Rebecca sipped her wine. "His best friend is over there playing pool. They're usually quite the team."

Charli peered over Rebecca's shoulder to the tables where a guy with shaggy brown hair was chalking up a pool cue.

"That wouldn't happen to be Roland Lierman, would it?"

"It is. You know him?"

"Not exactly, but I'd like to get to know him. Would you excuse me for a moment?"

"Yeah, of course." Rebecca kept a smile plastered on her face, but a flash of disappointment appeared in her eyes.

Charli was a little disappointed herself, to be honest. She and Rebecca had a lot to catch up on, but work always had to come first. This was a huge reason why Charli had such trouble maintaining friendships. What could she do when her job was so intensive?

As soon as Charli reached that side of the bar, Roland started shouting and waving his hands wildly. His untucked plaid button-down waved in the air behind him as he jumped up and down.

"And that's game! You owe me five grand, bro!" He pointed at a man in a navy business suit who appeared more than a little annoyed. "That's it, round of drinks on me! Hell, I'll get drinks for the entire bar!"

Charli wasn't even sure she heard right. Were they actually playing a game of pool for five grand? Was she still in Savannah or was this the twilight zone?

"Oh, hey, and I'll start by getting a drink for you first." Roland sidled up to Charli. He ran his fingers over his finely trimmed beard. "What are you drinking, pretty thing?"

She glanced down at the glass still nearly full of the bright green liquid. "I'm good right now." Charli kept her drink in her right hand, held far enough away that Roland couldn't reach. He didn't exactly seem like the kind of guy who was safe around open cups.

"Oh, fancy. I appreciate a girl with style."

Funny, because before this moment, Charli had never tasted Midori in her life, but she'd felt wrong ordering a beer at a place this nice. She'd heard the drink name on a television show. It was actually too sweet for her taste.

"I came over here to inquire about Bryce Mowery." There was no reason not to cut to the chase.

Roland groaned. "Don't tell me you're another chick hoping to hop on Bryce's junk."

So, not even Bryce's best friend knew he was dead yet? Interesting. Did that mean it was unlikely he had anything to do with his passing? Although talking about Bryce in the present tense could have been an act, Roland didn't seem smart enough to pull that off convincingly.

"No, I absolutely do not want to hop on Bryce's...junk or anything else."

"Then maybe you'll hop on mine." Roland's hand slid down Charli's back, grazing her butt before giving it a light squeeze.

Charli's reaction was swift. She didn't even have time to think about what she was going to do when she grabbed Roland's arm and thrust him toward the pool table. She even managed not to spill too much of her drink.

"Ow, ow, ow!" Roland whimpered as he tried to wriggle free.

Charli considered berating him but figured the embarrassment of being pinned down by a woman half his size was probably sufficient punishment. She doubted he'd be so brazen with another lady any time soon.

"Security, help!" Roland's voice had risen several octaves.

But the bouncer was walking over as slowly as possible, a small smile on his face. Roland was apparently just as hated as Bryce had been because a few women at the bar clapped in response to Charli's actions.

"Oh, give it up, you big baby." She let him go and flashed her badge. "You might want to reconsider who you fondle in the future. Got it?"

All the air seemed to go out of Roland, and he slumped against the table. "Yeah...sorry."

Setting her green drink down on the table, Charli headed toward the door. The guard fell into step beside her, chuckling as he escorted her out.

"Charli, hold up!" Rebecca scurried behind them, a paper in hand. "This is my number. I've really missed you. We should get dinner sometime."

With a smile, Charli took the small scrap of paper. "Yeah, we definitely should."

Charli stared down at the number as she walked to her car, squinting against the afternoon sun. Talking to Rebecca had caused little memories of Madeline to come back to her. The time they'd all gone swimming at Rebecca's house, teasing Becca about the ducky inner tube she wore. Or when Madeline spilled milk on herself at lunch and a few kids teased her for "peeing her pants" and Rebecca yelled at them all to back off.

The memories were painful, and reminiscing was bittersweet. But she never wanted to forget the time she spent with Madeline.

Maybe hanging out with Rebecca could help keep that part of her life alive.

7

"Yeah, thanks for your time. I'll definitely keep you in mind if I ever decide to buy goats and a couple of pigs."

Matthew hung up before the owner of a mom-and-pop hardware store could go off on another spiel about a product he didn't need. Nice enough guy. Overzealous with the marketing. Definitely didn't know his audience. Matthew's landlord was pretty laid back, but even he would flip his shit if one of his tenants turned their apartment into Old MacDonald's freaking farm.

He braced his hands in the small of his back and arched, groaning when his vertebrae popped. Three hours stuck in this chair was hell on his spine. Thirty-five years old and already falling apart. Not a good sign. Come forty-five, he'd probably be toddling around the precinct with one of those walkers they used in the old folks' homes.

He looked around the ugly hotel room. This sucked. First that gut-wrenching case with the dead teenagers, then Chelsea refusing to see him. Now, he was thousands of miles away from the one person who actually needed him, and he wasn't able to find a way to help her.

He'd started out with a solid plan. Matthew was going to identify the businesses that sold the exact type of ladder their killer used. Once that happened, they could ask to take a peek at the sales receipts for the past six months. From there, they'd generate a list of names and addresses of customers who'd purchased that make and model and then narrow it down to a small pool of viable suspects.

Theoretically, anyway. Generating a list only worked if the customer paid via credit card or check. For a cash purchase, they'd be SOL.

He faced his laptop screen and sighed. 'Course, at the moment, looked like he was gonna be SOL no matter what.

There were nearly sixty hardware stores within a hundred-mile radius of Savannah, give or take a few. Not too bad. The problem was the damn internet and online shipping. Nationwide, that number jumped up into the hundreds.

Twenty-six stores. That was how many he'd called, though it felt more like fifty. Some employees had accessed the information he'd needed lickety-split. Others had dragged the process on so long Matthew wanted to chuck his phone out the window. How many people needed to get on the line to find a stupid ladder? For one store, the answer turned out to be four. Four! Before an hour ago, he never would have guessed a hardware store would have four employees on the premises at the same time.

Every single one of them had asked the same questions too. "What are you looking for? Can you repeat the brand and model? Are you sure we carry that here?"

That last one killed him. The fourth time around, he'd finally snapped. "No, you absolute buckethead! That's why I've been sitting here talking to you clowns for the past twenty minutes so that you can look up the information and tell *me*."

When line had gone silent for so long, he worried they'd

hung up. The worker finally made a stilted apology and put him back on hold.

Almost ten minutes later, the first employee had returned to the line, breathless like he'd been running sprints. "I'm sorry, sir, but we don't carry that ladder size."

Matthew had pulled the phone away from his ear and stared at the screen. Were these people for real?

Twenty-nine minutes and thirty-two seconds. That was how long it had taken four people to figure out they didn't even carry an entire category of products. Unreal. He shuddered to think of how long he might have waited if he'd asked about an item they did stock.

Frustration had clenched his jaw, but he'd held back the acidic comments. Lately, the angry words seemed to come a lot more frequently.

He'd managed a terse "thank you" and hung up.

But on the off chance he ever did buy a home that he might need a ladder to do a little DIY on, he would definitely take his business elsewhere.

He shook his head as the irritation surged again. "Speedy Supply, my ass."

His phone rang. It was Charli. "Speedy Supply," he joked.

"What was that?"

"Nothing. I just checked the last store within my search radius. Twenty-six stores so far and only one carried a ladder of that make and model, but they don't stock that size. How about you?"

Charli blew a raspberry. "I'm partway through North Carolina and no luck yet. Oh, and I tried a couple of local discount stores, just in case, but apparently, that ladder is old, even though it looked to be in good shape."

"Now what?"

"Now you get to start calling stores in Tennessee and

Kentucky after you're finished with Georgia." Fingers tapped on a keyboard. "Just emailed you the list. Enjoy."

Matthew opened his email with a sigh. "Great. Looking forward to it." He settled back into his chair, mentally preparing himself for a couple of painful hours. "For all we know, he paid cash for them years ago out in California. What are the odds this leads us anywhere?"

Charli didn't miss a beat. "Better than the odds that doing nothing will lead anywhere."

"I wish you weren't right. Talk to you later."

They hung up, and he settled in to continue his calls. Another couple of hours ticked by before they regrouped and compared notes.

All in all, they'd located ten national livestock supply vendors who sold that particular brand, model, and size. After a little back and forth, eight of the vendors promised to hunt back through their order data for purchaser information and email the results as soon as possible. Another two said they'd have to call back the next day.

Matthew puffed his cheeks with air, releasing it again in a whoosh. "After all that, we only got hits on ten places, and who knows how long they're gonna take to get back to us?"

"At least we're making progress."

He smiled. "Well, aren't you just a little ray of sunshine."

Charli snorted. "Always." She was silent for a moment. "Matt, thanks for your help."

"You're welcome. Have a good rest of your day."

"You too."

His smile grew wider. He could just picture her, probably biting her lower lip. The no-nonsense, pixie haircut. The cute, slightly upturned nose. The strong, determined set of her chin and the intensity that pulsed off her in palpable waves. Not for a second did he begrudge her any of the good things coming her way. Charli was the bomb. She worked her ass off, and any advancement or accolade would be well-deserved.

No, the part that ate away at his insides like a vat of battery acid had nothing to do with Charli and everything to do with him.

Matthew opened up the mini fridge in his room and pulled out a beer. Maybe after a couple of beers, the sorry state of Matthew's own life would cease to matter so much.

8

Chester Crabtree's fingers shifted against the rubbery handle of his golf club. He kept his grip firm but relaxed, his eyes glued to the white ball shining in the bright afternoon sun. Metal clanked as he swung, sending the ball soaring over perfectly manicured green hills.

Rich Southerland put his hand to his brow, squinting against the radiant daylight to see where the ball had landed. "Not bad for someone who hasn't been out here for a month."

Chester usually had a few other country club members join him for rounds, but today only Rich was available at such short notice. One of Chester's appointments had canceled at the last minute, and he'd needed to get outside and swing his frustrations away.

"Well, you know, I've had a lot of business dealings to tend to. How's Alan liking college?"

"Sounds like he's having the time of his life." Rich stepped forward to line up his own shot. "He just joined our old fraternity, naturally. But don't think I don't know what you're doing here."

"What I'm doing?" Chester shrugged innocently.

"You're blowing past those mysterious business dealings you've got going on. Don't worry, I know better than to ask by now."

Chester let out a sly laugh. He didn't bother denying it. His old friend knew damn well that Chester didn't always stay on the right side of the fence. Not when there was so much cash waiting to be taken on the wrong side.

Rich swung, not getting his ball quite as far as Chester's.

Chester couldn't hold back a smirky grin. "Not bad for a guy who spends all day every day out here."

"Yeah, yeah, eyes on your own ball there, pal."

Chester laughed and headed to the golf cart to put his club away. He was just sliding into the passenger seat when another cart came racing up the hill. Chester squinted into the sun before recognizing the lone rider as another buddy, Ben Rymer. Good. The more the merrier.

Ben was red-faced by the time he stopped his cart next to them. Sweat poured down his temples. The man looked upset.

Chester reached into the cooler and tossed Ben a cold beer. "Who're you running from? Your wife again?"

Ben cracked open the can and downed half the brew before swiping the cold metal over his forehead. He inhaled deeply before meeting Chester's gaze. "Have you heard about Bryce Mowery?"

Alarm trickled down Chester's spine. "What about him?"

Ben looked at Rich and then back to Chester. "He's dead."

Rich was the first to speak. "Drunk driving again?"

Ben shook his head. "Rumor has it that the kid hung himself in one of Montgomery's barns."

Surprise nearly caused Chester to bark an inappropriate laugh. "You're shitting me?"

Taking another long swig of beer, Ben held up a hand.

"Not at all. Nobody is even supposed to know, from what my source at the police station told me. Montgomery's keeping it all hush-hush."

Chester shook his head. "Why?"

Ben shrugged. "From what I heard, Montgomery doesn't believe the kid would off himself. He thinks he was murdered. Had the GBI out to the farm and everything."

Rich and Ben kept talking, but Chester tuned them out.

Was it true? Had Montgomery really gotten the Georgia Bureau of Investigations involved?

Chester cracked open a beer for himself and half listened as Rich invited Ben to finish the game with them, but Ben declined. Chester managed to say the appropriate goodbyes before Ben took off, probably looking for another person to tell his secret to.

Rich pressed the gas, and the two of them rode in silence to where their balls had landed. The cart was previously in a shaded area, but the leather was still hot enough to cause beads of sweat to form on Chester's temple. Or was it the conversation with Rich that had him anxious?

Pulling the cart to a stop, Rich turned to Chester. "You've met Bryce. No way that kid killed himself."

Chester snorted. "He was hardly a kid. Wasn't Bryce thirty or so years old? And none of us really knew him. I see no reason it couldn't have been suicide."

Rich looked grim. "He was Montgomery's son. It doesn't get easier than that. Nah, I'm not buying it. With all those backdoor contracts Montgomery is always taking part in? He's pissed off many people in this town, people in high places."

Drawing in a heavy breath, Chester stepped out of the cart, turning so that Rich couldn't see his face. He didn't want his friend to note his unease. "Nobody's in a higher place than Montgomery, though."

"When you're at the top, there's nowhere to go but down. I've been waiting for the day that Montgomery stole a contract from the wrong guy. I'm telling you...this was revenge."

Chester tried to focus on which club to use, but he couldn't concentrate. "But Bryce? Why not attack Montgomery himself? It's not like Bryce was involved in the family business at all. There's no motive."

Chester knew better than this, but he also knew he was one of the few people aware of how Bryce was inching into his father's company. And he wanted to keep it that way. Even Montgomery himself didn't know what Bryce had planned.

Or did he?

"I don't know," Rich admitted, "but I still think this is Montgomery's past coming back to haunt him."

Rich was right about Montgomery's sordid history. His firm, like Chester's, never played by the rules. They'd get ahold of a property weeks before it was about to be safely labeled as historical and tear the bitch to the ground before anyone knew what was happening. Chester also knew that Montgomery involved himself with insider trading on the stock market that netted him an extra thirty grand a month. The man was shady as hell.

That wasn't why Chester hated Montgomery, though. He loathed that he could never keep up with him. It wasn't enough for Crabtree Industries to be the second most successful construction business in Savannah. Chester wanted to be first. He wanted to play the game better than Montgomery. And maybe after this incident with Bryce, he finally could.

"Well, I just feel bad for the family," Chester lied through gritted teeth. He couldn't let anyone know the contempt he held for the Mowerys, not even a good friend like Rich.

"Yeah, of course, me too. Montgomery Mowery is a nuisance, but I can't imagine how much of a mess I'd be if I ever lost Alan. That boy is my legacy. I know Montgomery feels the same."

"He was hoping Bryce would take over the business one day." Chester had to suppress a smile, knowing that could never happen now.

But the urge to grin faded quickly as he thought more about what Rich was saying. If Rich was already theorizing about Bryce, that meant others soon would be too. Chester couldn't have that. What if they found out what he'd done?

Grabbing the first club he put his hands on, he walked away from Rich before his friend could see his face. Chester had a lot of thinking to do.

Who else did he have to pay a visit to before things got out of hand?

9

C harli yawned as she parked in front of a large white home in the Historic District. She'd had a very busy Saturday with very little sleep the night before. All she wanted to do was go to her own home and curl up in her bed. Charli's own house wasn't very far away from this one, though this street might as well have been in a different world from her neighborhood.

Each house was a mini mansion. You'd never know these homes were built a hundred years ago. They all had perfect paint jobs and modern updates. Charli's home still had single pane windows that allowed both the heat and the frigid air to come and go as they pleased.

She had no earthly idea how a woman like Blair could afford a house like this. According to her records, the girl was only twenty-two. Barely a college graduate, what job would allow her to attain this level of luxury? Or was she still living at home? Or maybe she had inherited a healthy trust fund? Or, like Charli, the house could have been passed down to her by her grandmother.

Charli couldn't help but wonder if she'd also inherited a

death trap sofa like her own Priscilla. The thought made her smile.

Stepping gingerly toward the door, she followed the cobblestone path, careful to not put a toe out of line. Last thing she needed was a rich woman complaining that her gardener had to be called because Charli walked on the grass.

There was no doorbell, so Charli used the ornate iron knocker to announce her presence. When a woman came to the door, Charli's brow furrowed. The dark-haired lady in front of her had to be in her late forties. She certainly didn't match the profile photo Charli had found.

"Hello, I'm looking for Blair Daughtry."

"Blair is my daughter. May I ask your name?" She straightened out her perfectly ironed polka-dot dress.

Mrs. Daughtry was an image straight out of a 1950s magazine. If someone came up to Charli's door in the middle of an afternoon on a day she was spending at home, they'd find her in sweatpants with misshapen hair.

"I'm Detective Charli Cross." She flashed both her shield and a friendly smile. "I was hoping to have a moment to speak with Blair."

Blair's mom bit her lip. "Oh, no, what has she gotten into now?"

"It's nothing like that. Blair isn't in any trouble, but she may have information about a case I'm working on. Is she home?"

"Yes, she's out back by the pool. You can make a right and unlock the gate. It'll take you straight to her. Sorry, I'd invite you through the house, but I recently mopped."

Charli glanced down at the floor. It looked perfectly dry to her, but she didn't argue. "It's no problem at all, thanks."

Charli couldn't fathom an existence of mopping or doing other household chores in a freshly pressed dress. Then again, she'd never be a housewife to a man rich enough to afford this home.

The backyard was as well maintained as the front. The crystal clear pool was lined with crisp white lounge chairs, a few with umbrellas firmly planted for shade. But Blair was not sitting under an umbrella. She was sunning herself in a navy string bikini, the top unwrapped so she could tan without forming unseemly lines.

Somehow, she looked even more beautiful in person than she did in her profile photos. It was easy to see why Bryce dated her. Not only was she drop-dead gorgeous, but she maintained a lifestyle similar to him.

"Blair Daughtry?" Charli stepped across the edge of the pool to her.

"Yeah?" Blair didn't move, didn't even bother to take off her sunglasses.

"I'm Charli Cross, a detective with Savannah PD. I was hoping I could ask you a few questions about Bryce Mowery. You're his girlfriend, right?"

"His girlfriend?" Blair laughed and pushed up to her elbows. "Yeah, no, I'm not anyone's girlfriend. Bryce and I just hook up sometimes. Why? He's gotten into some kind of trouble?"

The media may not have published Bryce's death yet, but word was all over the precinct, and Charli knew it was only a matter of time before all of Georgia learned of Bryce Mowery's fate. Besides, she had a job to do. It wasn't often that Charli got to break the news of a victim's death to a potential suspect. There would be a lot of evidence in Blair's reaction.

"Blair, I'm sorry to have to tell you this, but Bryce has died."

Behind her sunglasses, it didn't appear Blair even batted

an eye. "Oh, how sad." Her voice was high-pitched and whiny but didn't convey any genuine concern. "How did it happen?"

"If you had to guess, what would you assume happened?"

It was a weird question for Charli to ask, and in any other circumstance, she wouldn't have. That kind of inquiry would trigger a grieving individual. But Blair obviously wasn't grieving. In fact, she appeared to be entirely unfazed.

"Probably a car accident? He loved to drive, and he was super reckless about it. Although that doesn't exactly explain why you're here." Blair's hand flew to her mouth in an exaggerated manner, almost like one of the actresses in those god-awful soap operas her mother used to love to watch. "Oh my god, he wasn't coming to my house, was he? That would be so tragic."

It didn't seem like Blair thought that was actually tragic, but Charli did get the vibe that such a story would make her feel somehow important. Maybe it was the kind of thing she'd write in her Instagram caption when she pretended to mourn Bryce online.

"No, he wasn't coming to see you. And it wasn't a car accident. He killed himself."

Blair's laugh was even louder this time. "Okay, seriously, how did it happen?"

"I'm very serious, Miss Daughtry. Bryce was found hanging in a stable near his house."

This elicited the first authentic reaction from Blair. "No way. He wouldn't do that. Bryce was a happy guy. I don't think I know anyone who was enjoying their life more. I'd sooner believe he murdered someone else than killed himself, no cap."

"No cap?"

Blair raised a judgmental eyebrow. "No lies."

Charli wasn't that much older than Blair but felt ancient

in her presence. They may as well have been from two completely different generations.

"It's interesting you bring up murder because I was going to ask if you knew anyone who wanted to harm Bryce."

Blair hummed to herself for a moment. "I don't know, maybe his girlfriend? Not that she seems violent or anything. But everyone knew Bryce was gonna dump her soon, and she clung to him like a needy golden retriever. You never know with those quiet ones. She acted all innocent, but like, she was dating Bryce so she was obvi a secret freak, if you know what I mean."

Charli didn't know but was too shocked to ask for clarification. Her mouth fell open slightly. "Wait, are you telling me that Bryce has a girlfriend...and she isn't you?"

"No, like I said, we're just hooking up. He was semi-kinda-maybe-official with Tanya Greenwood."

"And you know her? Did she know of you?"

Blair's pride shined through in her smile. "Yeah, definitely. She knew Bryce messed around with me and several other girls, but she wasn't bad enough to do anything about it."

Charli swallowed her judgment. What kind of person got this much satisfaction in being the other woman? It didn't matter. Charli didn't need to approve of Blair to get information out of her.

She pulled out her notebook and a pen that clung to her jacket pocket. "Give me all the info you have on Tanya Greenwood."

This was the first time Tanya's name had come up, but if Blair was right, and she seemed confident in her knowledge, then Bryce's girlfriend might provide more information than anyone else could.

10

Addington's Bar and Grill may as well have been extracted from the 1920s. Ornate wood paneling hugged the walls, leading up to the recessed ceiling with crystal chandeliers. Even though it was late afternoon on a Saturday, the waterfront establishment was quite busy. Every guest was dressed in at least business casual attire, making Charli stick out like a sore thumb.

She almost wished she taken a moment or two to stop by her house and change. After all, she'd only gone into the precinct this morning to finish the Marsh Killer paperwork. Had she known she'd been tossed another case so quickly, she might have tried a little harder when she'd gotten ready.

Maybe.

Or maybe not, since her current attire seemed to be working in her favor when a snooty looking man walked up to her with concern on his face. No doubt there was some kind of dress code Charli was breaking.

"Hello, do you have a reservation?" His tone was cordial, but his eyes exposed his judgment.

Charli squinted at the words under "Owner" on his name

tag. "No, Charles, I do not. I'm Detective Charli Cross." For the umpteenth time, Charli flashed her badge at another person. "I'm looking to speak to one Tanya Greenwood about a case I'm working on. Is she on shift today?"

His polite tone dropped as soon as he realized Charli was a cop. That wasn't an unusual reaction. A lot of business owners hated the optics of police walking through their establishment. That was especially true of a place as nice as this.

Charles smacked his lips together. "She is. If you step out back, I'll have her take her break and send her to you. Right through those doors."

Out back where they'd be out of view of the customers, but Charli didn't mind. Off to the right of the patio seating was a concrete wall hiding a POSIStation where servers could print out receipts and add their kitchen orders. Charli leaned against it as she watched the waves of the river lap against the deck.

The sun was getting low in the sky, and a wonderfully refreshing breeze was rolling through. Charli closed her eyes. The smell of garlic filled her nose as she allowed the lapping of the water to overtake the chattering of nearby guests. She could wait out here for Tanya all day. It was the most relaxed Charli had been in a good long while.

But Tanya was prompt. Her voice forced Charli's eyes open.

"My boss said you wanted to talk to me?"

"Yes, hello, Tanya. I'm Detective Cross. I'm here to talk to you about an investigation. Can we sit down?"

The young woman glanced around and gestured to a corner table. "This okay?"

Charli nodded and waited until they were both seated before breaking her bad news. "I'm here to talk to you about Bryce Mowery. I understand that you two have been dating."

"We have, yeah. Did he get arrested or something?" Her reaction to his name was drastically different from Blair's. There was no ambivalence in her expression. Tanya was worried.

Which only made what Charli needed to do more difficult. It was one thing to tell Blair about Bryce's passing when it was clear she couldn't care. Another thing entirely to have to break Tanya's heart in the middle of a busy shift.

"I'm very sorry to have to tell you this, but Bryce Mowery has passed."

The girl's face grew pale, and she blinked several times before shaking her head. "I'm sorry, what did you just say?"

Charli ripped the bandage off. "Bryce is dead, Tanya."

Either Tanya was an actress capable of an Oscar winning performance, or this was the first time she was learning of Bryce's death. Charli assumed she would have heard through the grapevine by now. The Mowerys' stranglehold on the information must be staggering.

Tears slowly filled the corner of her eyes. "How did it happen?" Tanya asked when she finally gained her composure.

Charli stood and picked up a white napkin from a stack of folded ones, handing it to the girl. "I'm afraid he killed himself."

"Oh, Bryce..." Her voice was soft.

"Do you have any idea why he might resort to suicide?"

She pressed the napkin to her eyes. "I mean, not really. I never would have expected this from him. But he certainly has been very overwhelmed lately."

Charli sat up straighter. "You're the first one to imply that Bryce wasn't happy-go-lucky every moment of his existence." Hopefully, divulging that little bit of information might make Tanya feel important, opening her up to sharing more. "You two must have been very close."

Tanya waved a hand in front of her face. "Well, yeah, we were. And happy-go-lucky was the image he wanted to portray. Don't get me wrong, he certainly liked to enjoy himself, but there was another side to Bryce. He really wanted to make something of himself. He'd been trying to follow in his father's footsteps, getting into the developing business. But it didn't take long for him to figure out that Savannah developers were all really shady and he didn't like some of the stuff he had to do to succeed."

"Like what?" Charli jotted down notes rapidly.

"He never told me any details because he didn't want me to be involved. Bryce said it was for my own safety. But I know he hated the sketchy things his dad had done. It was hard to look up to someone with such dirty hands."

"Bryce actually worked?" This flew in the face of every other testimony Charli had received. Even Montgomery Mowery painted a picture of a lazy hedonist.

"Yeah, absolutely. He'd been working hard. He'd been playing hard too, admittedly, but some of his partying was also related to business. He had to get in with other questionable people in order for some of his deals to go through. People like that do a lot of drinking."

"Do you know any of these questionable people?"

Tanya frowned, her fingers pulling at a loose stitch on the napkin. "I know his old friend Roland had been helping him with something. I was never told what exactly. And there was Aaron Eldridge. He'd met with him on Wednesday. Aaron is the kind of sleazy guy that always seems to know the dirt on every businessman in town."

Charli nodded, eyes glued to her notebook. "Know where I can find Aaron Eldridge?"

"I only know that Bryce said Aaron was leaving for New York after their meeting, but they were supposed to meet again on Monday. I think that's when he was due back."

If that was true, then the timeline made it unlikely that Eldridge was involved in Bryce's death. But if he knew about questionable business dealings around town, he was still a good interview candidate.

She made a note to check on Eldridge's travel plans.

"I have to admit, Tanya, I'm a little surprised to hear Bryce told you so much." Charli was debating whether or not to explain that she'd heard Bryce fooled around with many women.

Tanya seemed to know, though. "Because he didn't seem that serious about me, you mean? Bryce was a confusing person." Her eyes darted back and forth, like she was searching for the right words to say. "He couldn't contain his urges toward other women, but he still shared a personal connection with me. At first, I think he just liked slumming it with someone of a lower class, but we eventually became very close."

"And you didn't care about the other women Bryce was sleeping with?"

Charli couldn't fathom this. Not that she had a ton of experience in serious relationships, but she was damn sure that if her significant other was ever cheating on her, she'd drop him like a sack of old potatoes.

"I'll be honest with you. I was dreaming of the future. I wanted to marry Bryce. I cared about him, and he'd be able to provide me with a lifestyle I never had, so I looked the other way. I thought if he saw how easy I was as a girlfriend, he'd know how easy I'd be as a wife. I didn't care who he went around with, as long as I was the one he came home to. Although, obviously, that won't happen now…" Tanya's silent tears turned to heavier sobs. "I'm sorry, this is just a lot."

Charli nodded sympathetically but could not relate. The last thing Charli would want was to be tied down financially by any man.

"I understand. I have your information, so I'll contact you if any more questions arise, but I think I have everything I need for now. If you want, I can ask your boss to give you a longer break to compose yourself."

Tanya drew in a heavy breath and took the card Charli pushed across the table. "Thank you."

"No problem. And I'm very sorry for your loss."

Charli started to walk past Tanya when her hand shot out, grabbing Charli by the elbow.

"Detective, you should know, these construction and land development deals in Savannah are cutthroat. It's more competitive than you'd think."

Charli watched the young woman closely. "How so?"

Tanya's lower lip trembled. "Bryce likened it to war. A war he didn't know how to fight." Fresh tears fell. "And Detective?"

"Yes?"

Tanya leaned closer, lowering her voice. "Be careful who you question."

11

A wave of red splashed into Charli's wine glass, reminiscent of the waves of the river crashing into Addington's wooden patio dock. Unfortunately, Charli wasn't able to find the same peace from the river in her wine glass. Not with Tanya's words swirling around in her head.

Charli had been unsure about Bryce's death being a suicide, but she hadn't had a good reason why someone might want to harm Bryce, until now. To hear Tanya tell it, there was nothing a developer wouldn't do to get ahead in this town.

And before today, the competition within construction still wouldn't have made much sense in Bryce's death because nobody but Tanya believed Bryce did little more than party. Why would that be something Bryce kept secret? Was he more emotionally vulnerable than he wanted to let on? Afraid of what his father would think if he failed? Or were his business dealings simply so shady that he had to keep them under wraps?

And what the hell could be so shady about land development, anyway? Charli didn't get it. Sure, she could understand shady business practices from competitive business owners. But to make the leap from bribes or cutting corners on inspections to murder? That was a stretch.

The more Charli thought about Tanya saying that her boyfriend likened the business to a war, the more it made her think that Bryce was just being hyperbolic to impress his girlfriend. Nobody could make a mountain out of a molehill better than an entitled rich man. Maybe this so-called war was just a pissing contest among these development guys to cope with how boring their jobs were.

Charli walked her red wine into the austere sitting room. It was the only room in the house that still felt Victorian and classic. She didn't actually spend much time in it. Her library was in the living room, which was a candy-colored seventies style. Each room had its own decade, not a purposeful design choice, but something that had evolved over the years, thanks to Charli's eclectic grandma.

The house had been left to Charli when she passed, and Charli didn't have the time or money to change any of the decor. Even if she did, she liked that each room reminded her of her Grandma Carol. It was reminiscent of her childhood.

Still, of all the rooms, the living room was her favorite, but the John Wayne Gacy biography she wanted to read was in the sitting room. And after spending the day in gaudy bars and restaurants, it might be nice to enjoy the aesthetics of a space seeped in history.

Charli took a sip and grimaced at the taste. She wasn't a big drinker and wasn't really sure why she'd even poured the glass. A long hot bath would probably do a better job of taking the edge off her day, but the thought of running the water and then cleaning the tub afterward felt like too much work.

She set her wine atop a coaster on the side table next to the sturdiest chair. When in the sitting room, she always chose that chair, never the deathtrap of a loveseat her grandma had lovingly named Priscilla. Grandma made Charli promise to never get rid of the spindly thing, and she'd remained true to her word, but after falling twice as a child thanks to Priscilla's weak legs, she refused to sit in her again. Priscilla had caused enough trauma for a lifetime.

Charli pulled her legs in underneath her as she got comfortable with her book. The couch sat directly by the AC vent, which was just about the only thing in the entire house that worked well. A quick chill shot down her spine. A white knit throw was over one of the armrests, and she draped it over her body as she resumed chapter five.

A buzzing in her pocket stopped her from reading further. Matthew was calling.

"Hello?"

"Guess who's coming back to Savannah?"

Charli's grin faded when she realized this good news also meant that he'd given up on seeing his daughter. "When?"

"Flight leaves around noon tomorrow."

She wanted to tell him that she was sorry that his visit hadn't really been a visit at all, but she knew he wouldn't want her sympathy. "Ready to get back to work?"

"Yep. Can't wait to dig into this Mowery drama with you. What are you up to?"

"Definitely not reading a book about John Wayne Gacy."

Matthew groaned. "Don't you get enough of that at work?"

Charli couldn't help herself. Yes, she'd come across way too many psychos at her job, and she didn't much enjoy it. She certainly had no admiration for psychopaths, like the weirdos who started Ted Bundy fandoms on Tumblr. But forensic biographies still fascinated her endlessly.

Matthew didn't share her passion for psychological profiling, calling it a bunch of mumbo jumbo. But psychology was a science, and science could always be utilized in an investigation.

"I'd think you'd have seen enough death at work, yet here you are, binging on *Game of Thrones.*"

"Touché. So, anything new on the Mowery case? And are you really home? It's not even midnight."

Charli yawned. "Ruth sent me home after lovingly telling me I looked like shit. She told me to rest up tomorrow because she expected the press would be pounding on the doors come Monday morning." Charli set down her book and took the wine glass in hand. "Nothing definitive on the case, but I did see two of Bryce's lovers today."

"Two lovers, you say?" Matthew sounded incredulous.

"Oh, believe me, there's a lot more than two. But apparently one was Bryce's girlfriend, and the other was his flavor of the month. Even weirder, they both knew about each other and were perfectly fine with the situation. You weren't kidding about Mowery drama."

"Rich people are insane, I swear. If I had that much money, I'd be relaxing, not involving myself in any trouble."

"From the sound of it, that's not possible. I guess trouble is the name of the game when it comes to land development."

Matthew was quiet for several seconds. "What are you talking about, Charli?"

"Bryce's girlfriend told me that, although nobody else knew about it, Bryce had started becoming more involved in the development business, though he'd apparently been keeping his interest a secret from his father. She seemed to think there was a great deal of corrupt business practices in the industry. Apparently, Bryce told her that even his father had dirty hands."

"No joke. You think that had anything to do with Bryce's death?"

Charli sighed. "I don't know what I'm thinking, but I've

got to try every potential avenue for evidence. Soames said he won't have his completed report for at least another few days at least, but Tanya gave me a name of someone I want to interview. I'd love to know the other big names in development out here."

"On the flight, I'll work on getting a list of all current land sales and active construction sites logged with the city. We can go over it when I get back."

"That would be fantastic." Charli took another sip of her wine. "It's good to have you back."

"Good to be back. Can't wait to hear more lurid details about Bryce's romantic life."

Charli laughed. "I'll tell you everything I know, but it's probably not even the half of it. I…"

Charli sat up straight, struck with an idea. She didn't know the half of it, but it was possible to contact someone who did.

"Charli?"

"Shhh…I have an idea. Give me a second."

Matthew was quiet as she went into the entryway where her work jacket was hung on a black four-pronged coatrack. She reached into the pocket, pulling out the small piece of paper Rebecca Larson had handed her prior to exiting Olive's Lounge.

Rebecca had said she wanted to get together sometime. Would she be free tomorrow? It would be Sunday, so there was a decent chance.

"I bumped into an old friend at Olive's earlier today."

Matthew snorted. "You have an old friend?"

"Hardy har. I do, actually. A friend who hooked up with Bryce Mowery in the past."

"Hmm…you think she might know something?"

Charli shrugged, even though he couldn't see her. "Won't

know unless I give her a call. Let's chat more in the morning, okay?"

"Sure. And let me know how it goes."

"I will." She took in a deep breath. "And Matt?"

"Yeah?"

"I called my dad."

"You did?" His surprise rang over the line. "How did it go?"

She sighed. "We're having dinner tomorrow night."

12

Matthew sat under the robin blue sign of Mel's Juice Bar Sunday morning, patiently waiting for Charli to video chat with him.

He'd texted her an hour ago, hoping she'd fill him in on the case she was working. Plus, he was bored as hell. And frustrated. And sad.

His only kid hated his guts. And it was his own damn fault. He wasn't sure if he should just go home or try to see his daughter again.

One thing he was sure of was that he didn't want to spend another minute locked up inside a hotel room. He'd tried watching TV, but that'd gotten boring quick. Matthew liked to work. Was that really so terrible?

A light California breeze blew through his thinning hair. It wasn't too hot in the shade, no hotter than Savannah this time of year. Nobody else was sitting out on the patio, and in the solitude, there was a moment of peace for Matthew, something he seldom got to enjoy.

The spell was broken when his phone rang, and Charli's face appeared on his screen after he'd accepted the video call.

He laughed. She was sitting at a juice bar just down the road from her house.

He lifted his cup filled with strawberry banana, and a smiling Charli lifted what he knew would be pineapple mango. They "tapped" rims before taking long sips.

Charli moaned. "Pineapple mango. There's nothing better."

Matthew couldn't help but smile. He missed her face, missed the look she got when she first tasted a delicious meal. He'd never admit it, but the days were lonely without her.

There was very little left for Matthew in Savannah, at least, not anymore. There was a time when he came home to family. His wife would be cooking a hot supper, and his daughter would run into his arms as soon as he walked through the door. But that picture-perfect family devolved slowly over the years, finally ending when Matthew's wife cheated on him and then moved with her lover out of state.

Sure, Matthew had his part to play in their divorce. His job made him distant. He was never truly off-the-clock. It took a toll on his marriage. But unlike his wife, he was willing to work on things. He'd do anything to keep her and their daughter in his life. Now both Judy and Chelsea were on the other side of the country.

And now that he was on that side of the country too, neither wanted anything to do with him.

"You look well." Charli stared intently at him from his screen.

That was typical of Charli. It was the detective in her. Even within her interpersonal relationships, she was always looking for clues in body language or tone to assess a situation. Matthew would need to be careful about his response if he wanted to hide just how much he'd been struggling.

"I'm all right, just bored out of my mind."

And disappointed. So damn disappointed.

Charli took a sip of her juice. "You just chose a bad weekend to visit. Things will go better next time."

He wasn't so sure about that but shrugged noncommittally. "Yeah, it wasn't like I gave them any advance notice that I was coming, right? I just…" He wasn't sure how to finish.

"You just wanted to see your child." Charli's blue eyes were filled with compassion.

"Yeah."

And he'd needed to get away from his apartment. His home was a reminder of what this line of work had cost him. He was alone, his life dedicated to the precinct, and it was a thankless job. Matthew had spent little time over the past few years considering whether his dedication to his career was worth it, and he normally stayed busy so he didn't have time to reflect on it. He was afraid that if he dug deep, he wouldn't like what he found.

"Well, I understand how this job consumes your life." Charli took another sip of her smoothie, which was already half gone. "And, for the record, I hate doing this alone."

A warm flutter danced in Matthew's chest. The way his partner relied on him was the only thing lately that made the job worth it. Charli needed him, and he needed her…not like a lover, but like a big brother needed his little sis.

How a dad needed a daughter.

Geez. He needed to stop this line of thinking, or he'd end up sobbing in his own drink. He cleared his throat. "So, how are things going with the Mowery family? Have you figured out yet that I'm right, and the kid didn't kill himself?"

"I'm starting to." She shrugged. "I don't know. I don't have any definitive evidence of that, but something isn't adding up. When I went to Olive's Lounge to see what information I could collect, the picture that people paint of Bryce Mowery definitely is not consistent with a guy who would kill himself."

"Yeah?"

Charli shook her head. "And what I didn't mention last time we chatted was Bryce's dear friend Roland tried to grab my ass in front of the entire bar."

Matthew's eyes narrowed. "He did what?"

That was it. Matthew couldn't handle being so far away any longer. Fire raged in his eyes as he thought of any man daring to put his hands on Charli. Here she was, trying to do her job alone, and Matthew's absence was putting her safety in jeopardy.

"Relax, I put him in his place. Pinned him against a pool table until he was whining like a little baby for me to stop."

Of course she did. This cooled Matthew's fire just a bit.

He chuckled to himself. "Wish I could've been a fly on the wall for that moment."

"Well, the bystanders sure seemed to enjoy it. I don't think Roland is a popular presence at Olive's."

"Still, if I'd been there, I would have—"

"You would have tried to fight my battles like you always do?" Both of her eyebrows nearly touched her hairline. "Then I'm glad you weren't there."

"I don't do that." He poked his screen with his finger. "Like anyone could fight your battles for you. You're too stubborn to let them."

"Doesn't keep you from trying."

Damn right it didn't, and Matthew would do his best to defend Charli. She was a firecracker. He knew she could handle herself, but it wouldn't stop Matthew from feeling protective of her.

"I just wanna work this case with you." Matthew brought the straw to his mouth and a waterfall of strawberry and banana hit his tongue.

"Thought you'd rather watch *Game of Thrones* than be a lackey for Montgomery Mowery?"

"Well, I lied. I love the drama. I wish I could see the mess that is Bryce's friends and family. Don't get me wrong. As obnoxious as he was, the kid didn't deserve to die. But that doesn't mean I'm not interested in all his family secrets."

"You and the rest of the world, I'm sure. It's only a matter of time before the whole city starts creating conspiracy theories about what happened to Bryce Mowery."

A jingle sounded and Charli frowned. "I've got a call. I'll be right back." The screen went black, and Matthew sat back and took another sip of his drink.

She was back less than a minute later. "I'm sorry, but I've really gotta go."

"What was that about?"

Charli started walking, holding the phone so close to her face he could practically see up her nose. "My request for a background check just came back on Bryce's lover, Blair Daughtry. I've gotta run, but I'll call you with what I find out."

Matthew did his best to stuff down his disappointment. This quick chat with Charli was the most fun he'd had all morning.

All week.

All year.

Damn…he really needed to get a life.

13

The fresh smell of baking dough and melted cheese was causing Charli's stomach to do small flips. Until now, she hadn't realized how starved she was.

She'd barely eaten the day before and had skipped breakfast that morning. Well, unless she counted the smoothie she'd drunk earlier, which she didn't. Now, it was just a couple minutes until noon, and she was still suffering from intense disappointment that Blair Daughtry's background check had revealed a big fat nothing.

On paper at least, the girl was clean as a whistle.

Her phone buzzed with a text from Rebecca: *Running ten minutes late.*

Charli groaned and typed: *Still love supreme combo?*

The buzz came seconds later: *Still my fav!*

Charli practically leapt out of the red leather booth to place the order.

When she returned to the table, it was with two bubbly sodas in hand. Rebecca arrived not long after, though she didn't look as elated as when they'd run into each other at Olive's.

"Hey, how are you?" Rebecca smiled, but it didn't match her dejected tone.

Charli swallowed hard. "You heard about Bryce, huh?"

"It's all over town." Rebecca set her purse on the table, sliding into the booth across from Charli. "Was that what you came into Olive's about?"

"I'm sorry. I wanted to tell you, but his family hadn't announced it yet and I needed to be respectful."

"It's fine, I get it." Rebecca reached for her drink and took a sip. "It's not like I'm a friend or anyone close to Bryce, since hooking up briefly doesn't really count. I shouldn't even care. It's weird, you know? For some reason, hearing about a death always puts me in a peculiar mindset. Maybe you can't relate since you see death all the time."

It was weird how quickly she and Rebecca had picked up their friendship as if the past ten years hadn't even occurred. It was nice. There'd been no excuses or judgments, just the same closeness the two had shared before…

No. She didn't want to think about Madeline right then.

"I can absolutely relate to what you're saying, Rebecca, especially when it's an acquaintance who passed. I know you guys weren't close, but it's gotta be weird since you were hooking up with him not long ago."

"Exactly!" Rebecca shook her head, looking dazed. "I just can't believe he'd do something like this. He always seemed so free-spirited."

Charli's eyes shifted, making sure nobody else was close enough to hear them. "That's what everyone keeps saying."

Rebecca frowned. "What do *you* think?"

Charli would love nothing more than to spill her guts to someone she had a history with, but she needed to be careful. "That's what I'm trying to figure out. I could never divulge evidence to the public, but perhaps you could divulge some information to me."

She leaned forward, and that long strawberry blonde hair fell over her shoulders. Charli wasn't even sure what Rebecca did for a living, but she missed her calling if she wasn't a shampoo model.

"Are you going to grill me? Like in the cozy mysteries I read?"

Not quite, but Charli wouldn't burst her bubble.

"I'm just wondering if you could give me the rundown of everything you know about Bryce. I know you two weren't close, but any little detail you can give me would help."

Rebecca closed her eyes for a moment as she thought. "He wasn't very communicative before or after hooking up, I can tell you that. He definitely never told me anything personal. But I saw him around Olive's a lot. He would always go home with either Tanya or Blair, sometimes both. A little weird if you ask me."

"Were they the only two he'd run off with?"

"Oh, no, there were certainly other women. Sometimes, he'd leave with Roland or Aaron."

Charli reached for her notepad. "Aaron Eldridge?"

"Yep. I don't know much about him, other than the fact that he's definitely rich too. And they always seemed so hush-hush when they were together. With women in the bar, Bryce was loud and proud. But with Roland or Aaron, they'd be quiet as church mice while playing pool in the back."

Perhaps Charli hadn't given Roland enough attention in this case. He didn't seem like the type to ever keep his voice down. If he was doing so with this Eldridge character, maybe he was involved with Bryce's business.

"That's all I could really tell you, though. Sorry it's not more interesting. After our little hookup phase, Bryce hardly paid me any attention."

The pizza arrived at the table, cut into ten slices. The server set down two white plates, and though the pie was still piping hot, Charli wasted no time in pulling a slice onto her plate.

It was greasy as hell, just the way she liked it. There was no better pizza in Savannah than Gino's. Rebecca grabbed a napkin and carefully patted away the excess oil on top of the cheese. Blasphemy in Charli's eyes. Grease was the best part.

They were quiet for a moment as they both took their first bites. Mushroom, onion, sausage, and black olive exploded on Charli's tongue. A small moan of pleasure escaped her lips.

"That is damn good."

"Mmmm, reminds me of high school." Rebecca patted more grease off, and Charli tried not to watch. "Speaking of which, a lot of people from school have been talking about you catching that crazy serial killer. It's all over social media."

"Really?" Charli only had social media for her job. She never posted anything personal, and her information was locked down tight. She shuddered at the thought of sharing recipes and pictures of her meals with her old classmates.

"Everyone thinks it's so amazing what you were able to do for all those families. I can't imagine how hard your work is. Especially after, you know…"

And just like that, Madeline became the elephant in the room.

"You can say her name. It's fine."

Rebecca toyed with a string of cheese, wrapping it around her finger. "I didn't want to upset you. You two were so close, and you and her mother took it so hard. Do you guys still talk?"

"We didn't for a long while, but we recently spoke." A pang of guilt clawed at Charli's heart. "I'm going to do better."

"That's good. It's just so great to see you doing well for yourself." Rebecca's eyes glistened with unshed tears. "I used to worry so much about you, but you seem happy. You seem like you're doing what you love."

"I am. And honestly, it's thanks to her. I don't think I'd ever be in this line of work if it wasn't for what happened with Madeline."

To Charli's surprise, Rebecca reached out a hand, and the detective took it in her own. The two old friends shared a smile.

That terrible day still played on repeat in Charli's head. The look in Madeline's eyes as that man pulled her into his van would forever haunt her. How Charli looked away for just a moment to tie her shoe, only for Madeline to be stolen. She doubted she'd ever truly get over it.

Rebecca squeezed Charli's fingers. "She's proud of you, wherever she is."

Charli squeezed back, hoping that was true.

14

"*Choose.*"

The man's hand wrapped around her throat, tighter and tighter, cutting off her air as he dragged her through the graveyard. Charli gasped for breath while Spanish moss scratched her cheeks and yanked at her hair like invisible claws.

Choose what?

Her out-of-control heartbeat filled her ears, and in the distance, a girl laughed. Overhead, the Spanish moss slithered down from the trees like snakes, wrapping around Charli and trapping her arms to her sides.

Sweat poured down her back. She screamed, but the hand on her neck squeezed tighter, locking the words in her throat.

Drag, drag, drag. Her heels created trails in the dirt as the man kept pulling her back to the unknown.

Dread blanketed Charli like ash. Every step back cranked her terror up higher until she could taste the dusty-stale flavor on her tongue.

Something terrible waited for her back there.

He dragged her until her heels turned numb, past a wrought iron fence before dumping her beside a broken statue.

The woman jogger. Someone had toppled her to the ground and cracked off her face.

"Choose!"

Charli turned, and her heart stopped.

Sprawled in the dirt a few feet away was Madeline. Tears streamed from her friend's eyes, but she was alive. Madeline was alive.

Before her joy could bubble to the surface, the masked man was screaming again. "Choose!" This time, he shook Charli's shoulders and pointed. "Her or you."

Me. That was the word echoing in Charli's mind, but her brain malfunctioned. What came out instead was, "Her."

No! She shook her head, desperate to fix the mistake. *No! Not her, me! I meant to say...me!*

Only, this time, no sound came out. Panic flooded every cell as the man grabbed Madeline around the neck and began dragging her away.

Charli lurched to her feet to crawl after them, only to trip and fall. Her stupid shoelaces were messed up again. Tangled into hundreds of tiny knots. Fear turned her fingers to rubber as they yanked at the snags.

Come on, hurry!

A bone-chilling laugh pulled her head up from the task. Just in time to see Madeline's face.

Her friend's terrified expression had twisted into one that seethed with malevolence. "Liar, liar, pants on fire. Told me you'd find him, but you never both-ered..."

The high-pitched, singsong tone was both Madeline's and not. Both innocence and evil.

"No! I didn't lie, I swear!" Charli gave one last desperate tug on the laces, but they wouldn't yield, and no amount of clawing could pull the shoes from her feet. By the time she gave up, her ankles dripped blood.

Gasping, she somehow managed to stand and hobble a few steps *forward.*

"Madeline, wait! Take me instead!"

The next step, she plunged into a deep hole, landing at the bottom in a thick layer of marshy mud.

She fell on her back, panting for breath.

Get up! Move. You need to save Madeline.

Charli struggled to sit while, within the darkness, a shape flickered to life. She scooted backward as an awful, rotting meat reek filled her nose.

As she gagged on the stench, two corpses pushed themselves from the earth. Maddie's face was half rotted off, while Madeline's was nothing but a skeleton.

"You should have saved us..."

Before Charli could react, both of the rotting Madelines opened their skeletal jaws and began to scream.

Charli jerked awake with a scream. A second later, the alarm on her phone sounded and she screamed again. Heart racing, she plopped back on her couch, cursing herself for falling asleep. It was a good thing she'd set a reminder on her phone. She was having dinner with her father.

She groaned. She wasn't even all that hungry after her lunch with Rebecca.

That must have been what prompted the nightmare. Seeing one old friend had made her think of another, and then her subconscious had tossed in the teenager who was murdered on her last case.

Charli closed her eyes, forcing her mind from them both. Right now, she needed to get ready to see another blast from the past...her dear ole dad.

AN HOUR LATER, Charli pushed open the front doors to MoMo's and was greeted by pop music and the spicy scent of garlic and buffalo sauce. The restaurant was bustling, packed with people her age and older, ending the weekend with happy hour drinks around the horseshoe-shaped bar.

Her dad rose from a cushioned bench in the waiting area. She gave him a quick hug before stepping back.

Relief loosened a knot in her stomach as she performed a quick inventory. Same thick dark hair with a faint sprinkling of gray, same alert blue eyes, still as fit as ever. He appeared none the worse for wear since the last time they'd met up. "Have you been here long?"

"No, only about fifteen minutes or so."

"Fifteen minutes? Dad, I told you to go ahead and let them seat you if you got here early. That way, you could at least order a drink while you waited."

Jason Cross waved her off, just like he did every time she made the suggestion. "What do I care if I order a drink sooner or later? Besides, this way I get to see my beautiful daughter the second she walks in." He ruined the sentiment a moment later by adding, "Let's face it, I see you so infrequently that I need to appreciate every minute I get."

Charli groaned. "Really, Dad?"

He winked at her. "Aw, come on, just a little joke."

Yeah, right.

As they followed the hostess to a booth in the back, Charli decided not to argue. She had promised herself that she'd try harder not to let her dad ruffle her feathers this time. Sure, his teasing got old sometimes, but wasn't that what dads were for? At least he was smiling. That was a good sign.

A waitress stopped by their table within seconds of them sitting down. Charli ordered a sweet tea and her dad a caffeine-free root beer, and they ordered six buffalo wings and six sweet and spicy Thai-style wings to share.

Once the waitress left, her dad started grinning. Charli narrowed her eyes. "What?"

"Oh, nothing. I just remembered the time when you were a kid and insisted on ordering the extra spicy habanero wings. Do you remember that? Nothing your mother or I could say would dissuade you. Some punk at school was running around saying he could only eat a single bite because they were so hot, and you got a bee in your bonnet that you needed to prove him wrong. What was his name again?"

Charli winced. "Sean Marcus." His was a name that lived on in her memory. They'd been in fifth grade at the time, and Sean had spent the last two years pegging her in dodgeball every time his hands touched the ball, laughing about how she'd never beat him at anything.

She'd been determined to make him eat his words. Even if the one sport she kicked his butt at involved chicken wings.

Her dad snapped his fingers. "Sean Marcus, that's it. You remember that whole incident?"

"How could I forget? I seriously thought I was going to die for the first thirty seconds or so. It was like someone opened my mouth and poured in liquid fire. And you and Mom were sitting there trying to act all serious, but you kept giggling like some kind of sadist who enjoyed the sight of his daughter in pain. Just like you are right now."

She pointed at his face, which only made him laugh harder. "I'm sorry, but those noises you were making sounded like a moose during mating season. And your face, oh man," his shoulders shook, "I've never seen a kid turn that bright red before without a sunburn. You looked like the kid from that Gene Wilder movie. You know, the one with the little orange people who worked for free in his candy shop?"

"*Willy Wonka and the Chocolate Factory*. And you're telling me I looked like an Oompa Loompa?"

"No, not them, like that bratty girl who turned into a blueberry...except you looked more like a beet."

"I bet you don't even know what a moose during mating season sounds like." Her attempt to appear indignant was lost when she started giggling too. She remembered her dad's coughing fits, which she later figured out were his unsuccessful attempts to hide his amusement. Her mom, on the other hand, had managed to keep a straight face the entire time. "At least Mom didn't laugh."

"Ha! That's what you think. Remember when she jumped up from the table to go get a pitcher of water? You were probably too busy regretting your life choices to notice that your mom was cackling like a witch."

Charli's mouth fell open. "What? No way."

"Oh, yes way. Your mom had more discipline than I did, sure...but mostly, she was quicker on her feet."

The image of her mom racing from the table to keep from busting out laughing filled Charli with an odd sort of joy. "I guess I was a pretty strong-willed kid, huh?"

The waitress delivered their drinks, and her dad sipped the root beer while lifting his bushy eyebrows. "You, a strong-willed kid? What makes you say that?" He winked. "Lucky for everyone, you outgrew that trait fast."

His wry delivery made Charli smile again. "Yeah, well, I wonder where I got that from?"

"Your mother, definitely."

She snorted. "Please."

While munching on wings, they chatted about the latest hijinks of her dad's dog Loki—he'd always been a huge Marvel fan, and Thor's adopted brother had been her mom's favorite character—and how his across-the-street neighbor had finally convinced him to take up Zumba classes. The more they talked, the more her guard lowered and allowed hope to bloom in her chest. Everything was going so well that she kicked herself for having reservations in the first place.

She'd spent too many hours since her mom died drowning in pessimism over their volatile relationship. Several times, she'd even wondered if it was DOA, with no remaining hope of resuscitation. She'd told herself she'd be okay either way. People grew estranged from their families all the time and ended up no worse off.

Seeing his familiar, smiling face across the table brought that ridiculous notion crashing to the ground.

This was her dad. The man who'd carried her through parades every year on his shoulders so she could see all the floats. The person who'd helped her with her math homework without complaint. The parent who'd held her while she'd sobbed on the living room couch in front of a sitcom, hours after everyone left from her mom's wake.

She'd be heartbroken if they kept squabbling until they finally stopped speaking at all. Thank goodness they were getting along better tonight. This could be the start of a new path forward for them, one where they didn't pick at each other until one of them bled.

Charli was scrubbing her messy hands on her napkin after polishing off a second wing when her dad's face turned pensive. "I left lilies on your mother's grave two days ago. Sometimes, it's hard to believe she's been gone this long, and other times, it seems like it was just last week that she was sitting across from me at the dinner table, scolding me for slipping Loki bites from my plate."

The smile froze on Charli's face. Lilies. Two days ago.

Her mind flashed to the calendar on her phone, and her heart plummeted. Guilt was a pair of iron jaws clamped onto her ribs. "I forgot Mom's birthday."

Her dad shrugged and tossed a clean bone into a bowl. "Not like it's some big surprise. You don't seem to remember much outside of your job anymore. Although, hey, you did show up tonight, so that's something."

Charli dropped her gaze to her plate to hide the sudden sting of tears. She should have known better. No matter how well things between her and her dad started out, this was how they always ended, in a regurgitation of this exact argument.

Maybe her dad had a point. She couldn't believe she'd forgotten about her mother's birthday.

She dragged her glass closer and sucked several gulps of tea down through the straw, hoping the liquid would help loosen the giant lump lodged in her throat.

Once she managed to do that, her guilt was joined by a deep, simmering heat. Why couldn't her dad just support her job for once? Was it really that hard? "I'm sorry that I missed Mom's birthday. I've been swamped at work with a big case that's—"

"There's no need to explain. There's always a big case with you. Are you ever going to take some time off for yourself?"

Not this again.

"Believe it or not, bad guys aren't very considerate when it comes to my personal life. But when I catch the next one, I'll be sure to share your complaints." She swiped the napkin angrily over her mouth before wadding it into a tight ball. "Did it ever occur to you that maybe, just for once, that I'm doing something worthwhile, and instead of raking me over the coals every time we meet up, you could, oh, I don't know, be proud of me?"

Her dad dragged a hand down his face. "Oh, come on, you know that has nothing to do with anything. Of course I'm proud of you."

"Really? Because it doesn't show." She pushed her plate

away, her appetite gone. "Mom always supported my career goals."

She murmured the words, more to herself than anything, but her father bristled.

"She did, but I can tell you right now she never would have wanted to see you turn into this...workaholic that you've become, constantly running yourself ragged at work at the expense of the rest of your life. And for what? So you can keep making amends for Madeline's death?" He pounded the table with his open palm, making the plates rattle. "When is it going to end, Charli? When is enough, enough?"

Charli snapped back without thinking. "When I find her killer. That's when!"

The declaration smothered her dad's fire. When he gazed at her across the table, he suddenly showed every bit of his fifty-nine years. "Oh, Charli."

He shook his head like he wanted to say more. Her phone cut him off when it started to ring.

Still reeling from their argument, Charli glanced at the screen. She didn't recognize the number, but she needed to take the call anyway. She didn't have the luxury of screening her calls. Any of them could be important. "Excuse me. I've got to take this."

She jumped to her feet, ignoring her dad's grumpy, "Of course you do," as she headed for the back hallway that housed the restrooms.

"Hello? Hang on just a second. I'm getting to a quieter spot." She scooted inside the bathroom and locked the door, pressing her back against the cool wood and closing her eyes. "Okay, go ahead."

"Hello, this is Wayne Lawrence from WTCB, and I'm hoping you can give me update on the recent death of Bryce Mowery."

Seriously? How did a reporter get her personal cell number? And why was she more excited to talk to a reporter than her father?

"Sorry, I'm unable to speak about an ongoing investigation."

"But Bryce's father, Montgomery Mowery, insists that his son was murdered. Can you comment on that?"

Charli closed her eyes. "Please lose this phone number and use the proper channels for any press releases. I'm sure you know the number of the press office."

"But—"

Charli ended the call before another word was said. She then blocked the number, and sat on the toilet for a few minutes, taking deep breaths. When the woman in the next stall farted, she decided it was time to leave. She escaped the stall and moved to the sink to wash her hands in extra hot water. Twice.

Feeling calmer and ready to face her father again, she strode with as much confidence as she could muster to their table.

Her dad took one look at her expression and groaned. "Let me guess…duty calls, and you have to leave."

She opened her mouth to say that wasn't the case, but the look of mild disgust stopped her.

Why was she putting herself through this?

"Actually, I do."

He snorted. "Figures, but don't worry, I'll grab the check…of course."

Bristling from the top of her head to her heels, Charli opened her bag and pulled out her wallet, tossing two twenties on the table. She was an adult capable of making her own life choices.

She gave him the best smile she could muster before turning toward the door. "My treat."

15

"That was a quick trip." Ruth's voice rang through the empty hallway behind Matthew.

The sergeant finding him moments after he entered the door was no surprise. The woman seemed to have eyes in the back of her head. "Yes, ma'am, and I'm ready to get to work."

Ruth nodded toward the staircase that led to his office. "Then you better get to it. I want some answers on the Mowery case today."

Matthew let out a relieved sigh when he stepped in the space he and Charli shared. The stale office air had never smelled so good. The unique aroma of printer ink and overheated computers was better than the lingering yeast from empty beer bottles that littered Matthew's hotel room.

"You're back." Charli brightened as she stepped through the doorway.

"Sure am. Do I get a hug for it?"

Charli sighed dramatically. "I guess just this one time won't hurt."

Her tiny body curled around his mighty frame, and if he

closed his eyes, he could almost believe it was Chelsea in his arms. They were about the same size, after all.

When Charli dropped her arms, Matthew cleared his throat and moved over to his desk. "So, I've got that list ready for you. There aren't as many construction companies in Savannah as I thought there would be. Who do you want to start with?"

"How about Roland Lierman?"

"Uh, don't think he's on my list." Matthew looked down at the printed paper, scanning for the name.

"He's not. He's the guy who grabbed my ass at the bar, remember?"

"Oh, right. Well, then, I definitely want to pay him a visit." Matthew cracked his knuckles. "Probably not for the same reasons you do, though."

Charli laughed. "Definitely not for the same reason. I think I need to question him further about how he was involved in Bryce's business dealings. We can stop by his house first and then go down the list and ask whoever we can find about the Mowery family. I've already called around to a few companies and have been told the owners should be available to meet with us."

"Sounds like a plan. You driving?"

"Yep. I just need to pull up his address and..." Charli paused as she opened her phone.

"What is it?"

Charli moaned. "A text from my dad berating me for leaving dinner early. Same as usual."

After all these years working with Charli, his partner had rarely spoken about her father. Nobody could keep their cards closer to the chest than Charli could. Even when you thought you were close to her, you'd find there were endless personal details she was hiding. She was the most impartial person Matthew knew, but also extraordinarily closed-off.

Maybe that was why Matthew was so drawn to her. In many ways, his ex-wife was also very detached. Matthew was attracted to a closed book he had to pry open. Not that he wanted to dig into Charli's life for personal reasons. He could never see his partner that way.

Matthew examined the area when they arrived at their destination. Roland Lierman's house was in a well-to-do neighborhood, but it was unusually small compared to the rest of the homes.

"Why would he pay a premium for such a tiny house in this neighborhood when he could have a home twice the size on the other side of Savannah?"

Charli shrugged and exited the car. "Maybe for the same reason he surrounds himself with people like Bryce. He wants to live a certain lifestyle, run in elite circles, even if he wasn't born into wealth."

"True." Matthew nodded and headed toward the sidewalk.

Charli grabbed his arm, pulling him back. "Let me be the one to knock, okay? I can't wait to see his face when he realizes who I am."

He waved for her to go ahead of him. "Be my guest. I'm eager to see that too." Matthew still desperately wished he'd been there to see Charli give the beatdown on this kid. It cracked him up when she got feisty.

When the crimson door opened, Roland's jaw nearly fell to the floor. It was a far more dramatic reaction than Matthew was expecting. Charli must have done a real number on him.

"What are you doing here?" Roland took a step back, as if Charli might lunge at him at any moment.

"Nice to see you again, Roland. I'm Detective Charli Cross. This is my partner, Detective Matthew Church. I trust that if I come in, you're going to keep your hands to yourself?"

Matthew didn't think Roland's eyes could grow any wider, but they practically bulged out of his head. "Wait, you're really a cop?"

"Sure am. Are you going to be gracious and invite us in?"

"Uh, s-sure."

Roland stepped inside, letting Charli walk in first before Matthew followed. Matthew glared at him, refusing to allow Roland even a modicum of comfort. He wanted to intimidate Roland for how he'd treated Charli, but he wouldn't say anything out loud. If he did, it would be him who had to deal with Charli's wrath next. He didn't need that on his first day back. Charli was constantly reminding Matthew that she was independent enough to take care of herself.

"This is a lovely home." Charli invited herself to walk farther into the house, passing the living room and entering the kitchen.

Roland thrust his hands into his pockets. "Thanks."

"What do you do to afford a place as nice as this?" Charli raised both eyebrows.

Roland cleared his throat. "I dabble in the stock market some."

"That's not exactly a career, though, is it? I mean, you need money to invest before you can enter into the market. Surely you have another job." Matthew stepped in front of him, wandering into the dining room.

"I also have a company that builds an online presence for new start-ups. Social media ads, web design, stuff like that. A lot of my investments came from that, but I've also been gifted stocks from friends."

Matthew highly doubted this was all that Roland did. But they weren't there to bust him on whatever petty crime he was involved with.

Charli pulled out a pen to take notes. "What work have you conducted with Bryce Mowery?"

"None." The answer was quick. Almost too quick. "I mean, he'd sometimes ask for business advice, but I never understood why when Montgomery would've been better to talk to."

Charli gave Matthew a knowing look, and he wondered what she was up to. He didn't have to wonder long.

"Are you telling me there's no financial reason you'd want to see Bryce Mowery dead?"

It was a bold question, an accusation meant to draw out a greater reaction from Roland. Matthew usually played bad cop in interrogations like these, but Charli obviously wanted to have her fun with the asshole who thought he could grab her ass in public.

"What? Hell no! Bryce was my buddy. I stayed over at his house, like, every other weekend. I'm devastated about what happened."

"Yeah, you look like it." The words practically dripped with sarcasm.

"I am!" Roland held up both hands. "Look, it's hard for me to cry around other people, all right? But I'm sad as hell. I don't know what I'm gonna do without him."

"What kind of things would you and Bryce do when you hung out?" Matthew leaned against the marble kitchen countertop.

"I dunno, go out drinking. Played a lot of video games at his place. We just chilled."

"Chilled." Matthew drew the word out into several syllables. "When you were 'just chilling,' did Bryce ever tell you about moving into the land development business like his father?"

"Yeah, of course. He'd been trying to work out a couple of deals. He kept it under wraps because he didn't want his dad hearing about it. Bryce was hoping he would be able to come to Montgomery with a killer deal and show him how much of a badass he was."

"Was there anything specific he told you about? Any recent deals he was working on?"

Roland shook his head at Charli's questions. "Nah, not that he told me. I mean, he said he had something in the works, but he was super secretive about it."

Charli looked up from her notebook. "Did you think that was odd?"

"Not really. Those development guys are always like that. They act like if they even whisper about a deal, it'll all fall apart. I didn't expect to hear about anything until it was finished."

Matthew fired off the next question. "You're friends with other people in land development, then?"

"Just Aaron."

Charli perked up. She knew the answer but asked the question anyway. "Aaron who?"

"Eldridge."

She wrote it down like it was new information. "What can you tell us about him?"

Roland scoffed. "Aaron is a character. He plays all secretive about his deals until he's finished, and then brags to everyone in town. He got rich overnight. Some estranged family member, an uncle or something, died and left Aaron his riverfront property. I think there may have been something in the will excluding Aaron from selling it, but that didn't stop him. He made a fortune off that land. Now he's trying to start his own construction company or some shit like that."

Matthew pulled out the printed paperwork detailing active construction sites in the area. "Is that along the Ogeechee?"

"Yeah, not far from here. Why?"

Matthew looked over at Charli. "It's on my list of active developments."

She grinned. "Guess we know where we're headed next."

Charli stepped in front of Matthew, and when her back was turned, Matthew ran a finger across his own throat in a cutting gesture. The message was understood clearly because Roland turned red and looked at the floor.

If Charli had seen the gesture, she would've chastised Matthew about how she could fight her own battles. But what she didn't know wouldn't hurt her.

16

"I thought you said there was supposed to be active construction here?" Charli shut her car door as she stepped onto the lush grass. "Are we at the right place?"

Matthew looked as confused as she felt. "Definitely. I guess they haven't started up yet."

Although it didn't appear there was much to see, the pair still walked along the empty strip of land running adjacent to the Ogeechee River. Despite it being midday, it felt cooler out by the water.

"Imagine your house backing up to this view." Charli waved her hands in a large circle.

"I can't. I don't let myself imagine stuff like that. I'll never be a millionaire."

Matthew wasn't exaggerating. If this area was going to be used for a housing development, each home would go for several million easy. Savannah wasn't generally an expensive place, not for housing or other living expenses, but that changed once you reached the waterfront properties. And untouched riverfront land like this was extremely rare in Savannah. It likely sold for an obscene amount.

"Yeah, me either, but it's fun to fantasize." Charli glanced over at Matthew, who had his hands in his pockets.

"Not for me, not anymore. I realized fantasies are just an obstacle to happiness, a lie we tell ourselves when we're not content with our current life." He kicked at a rock. "Used to tell myself that, one day, my work would slow down. One day, I'd get to spend every evening with my wife and daughter. I only had to wait for that day."

Matthew's eyes shifted to Charli, and then his head jerked away. He clearly hadn't meant to divulge so much.

"You okay?"

"Yeah, yeah, I'm great." Matthew laughed awkwardly. "Just too much time to think while I was away. Damn good thing I'm back, huh?"

This part of Matthew, the one that worked away his pain, was the part Charli most deeply related to. Perhaps it was the center of all workaholics' lives. Charli hadn't gotten promoted at such a young age for nothing. She'd foregone all the fun, carefree time of her early twenties to invest in her work.

And while she loved her job, passion didn't drive her forward. She gave up on a social life, on relationships, on hobbies because she genuinely didn't want those things. She avoided the truth as much as possible, but it still lingered in the air during every quiet moment. If Madeline didn't get to have that life, Charli wouldn't, either.

Matthew kicked another rock. "So, what do you wanna do, head on back to the precinct?"

"You know what? Let's just keep walking for a bit. It's nice by the water. No reason we can't recount details of the case out here instead of the office. I could use the fresh air."

Charli couldn't pinpoint why, but this suggestion appeared to make Matthew slightly uncomfortable. Still, he agreed. "I suppose we can do that."

"You suppose? What is it? Did you get too much time away from the office and now you're dying to go back?"

Matthew smiled. "You caught me. So, what did you think of Roland?"

Charli moved forward on the tall grass, fully enjoying the river views. "He isn't involved with Bryce's death. Not directly, anyway."

Matthew squinted at her. "How are you so sure?"

"Because he spoke about Bryce in the present tense Saturday at the bar. The man is too dumb to act that well."

Matthew let out a slow, drawn-out chuckle. "Wait a second. You were positive that he wasn't involved when you gave him that harsh line of questioning?"

Charli shrugged. "Yep, just wanted to make him as uncomfortable as possible."

"Well, you succeeded. That's for sure."

Charli tripped and nearly landed on her hands and knees but managed to stay upright. "Crap."

"You okay?"

She waved the question off and searched for whatever had caught her shoe. It was a plastic sign with flimsy metal stakes that hadn't been successful in keeping it in the ground.

"What's this?" She grabbed the yard sign. Bold black font stood out on a lime-green background reading "Crabtree Industries."

"Ah, yeah, they're listed as the company handling construction out here. The company is owned by Chester Crabtree."

"Is he as rich as Montgomery Mowery?" Charli tried to stuff the sign back into the same hole it came out of, but the dirt must have shifted because it fell flat.

Matthew took it, moving it a few inches backward before stabbing it into the earth. "He's close, that's for sure. I think his business and Mowery's run pretty neck and neck."

"I wonder if Mowery Senior made a bid on this property and Crabtree won out."

Matthew side-eyed Charli. "I'm sure he tried to get it, knowing what this land is worth. But so what? Does that really matter to us?"

Charli glanced up at him, holding his gaze. "Maybe."

Matthew opened his mouth but didn't speak when Charli's phone rang. Soames was calling.

"Detective, I hope one day to give you a call for a pleasant afternoon chat, but I'm afraid today is not that day."

Charli couldn't hold back her laugh. Even in the darkest of situations, Soames had a way of making everything feel lighter. It was a gift that came with being a medical examiner, she supposed. When surrounded by death daily, there wasn't much that could bring you down.

"What do you have for me?"

"We processed both the rope that Bryce was hanged with and the rope Montgomery verified he purchases for farm use. They were not made of the same material. The rope that hung Bryce is derived of hemp, cotton, and sisal."

Charli thought through the possibilities. "Okay, a little suspicious, but couldn't he have bought that rope elsewhere and brought it to the farm?"

"He could have. Except none of those materials were found on Bryce's hands. We found a lot of it on his neck, of course, but there is nothing to suggest that Bryce himself actually handled the rope."

Charli bit her lip and glanced over at Matthew. "So, Bryce could not have done this himself?"

"No. I mean, if you were to go with an outlandish theory, he could have used gloves to touch the rope before he hung himself. But why would anyone about to commit suicide do such a thing? And furthermore, we searched the stables high and low. There were no gloves to be found except those located in cabinets or drawers. Someone else had to be there when Bryce died, and most likely, forced him into this situation."

Matthew looked about ready to hop out of his own shoes. "What? What's he saying?"

Charli was about to explain to him when Soames spoke up again. Before he did, she put him on speakerphone. "There is something else."

"What's that?"

"When we examined the rest of Bryce's body, we found a break in his wrist. It was a recent injury. If I was a betting man, I'd lay odds that it happened the night of his death."

"I know better than to make bets with you. Any idea how it happened?"

"The break is consistent with a fall, but not likely that Bryce fell of his own volition."

"Wait, but how could you know that? Wouldn't a break from a fall look the same regardless of whether Bryce fell himself or was pushed?"

"Usually, yes. But in this case, the break occurred in the opposite direction you'd expect if Bryce were to catch himself on the ground. It looks like he hit the back of his hand first, bending his wrist inward. Normally, when someone has an accidental fall or is pushed, they will splay their hands out to catch their own body. Bryce wasn't able to catch himself. There is a possibility that he could have been dazed and fading out of consciousness by the time he hit the ground. Which would make sense considering the contusion on his right temple."

It took a moment for Charli to process this. "Are you saying someone hit Bryce in the head, and he was disoriented when he fell?"

"It's a theory based on the evidence before me, and that scenario would be consistent with this kind of break, yes.

Unless Bryce was so severely intoxicated that he wasn't able to catch his own drunken body. But toxicology showed his blood alcohol content at only slightly above normal. He was tipsy, but not drunk enough for that kind of fall."

Matthew was still looking at Charli with eager eyes. He mouthed the words "you were right."

"Still there, Detective Cross?"

"Yes, I'm here."

"One last thing for now. I examined the heels of the victim's shoes as you suggested, and I agree with your theory. The shoes appeared to have only been worn a couple of times, yet the backs of the heel area were scratched significantly whereas the rest of the leather was relatively unflawed."

Charli had known it in her gut. "He was dragged."

"It appears so. Under a microscope, small particles of gravel and dust suggest that he was dragged on a gravel road. I'll send over all the forensic data I have, but we're officially changing the cause of death from suicide to homicide."

Charli may have suspected this was coming, but getting the official cause of death still put her in a different headspace. It was no longer a question of *if* Bryce was killed, but by whom.

17

"You ready for this?" Matthew stood poised to ring Montgomery Mowery's doorbell, waiting for Charli's go-ahead.

She took a deep breath. She'd lost the hand of blackjack they'd played after getting the report from Soames. A quick game had become their tradition whenever they needed to break bad news to a family. The loser was the one stuck with crushing another person's heart.

Although, this time, what they needed to share might not even constitute bad news. Right now, their disclosure of a murder might actually come as a relief. Mowery had been insistent that his son didn't kill himself, and though it wouldn't bring Bryce back, the truth would likely bring a wave of comfort.

"I'm good to go." Charli put her hand in front of Matthew to ring the doorbell first.

Montgomery answered within seconds, his eyes eager and anxious at the same time. "Detectives, do you have some news about Bryce?"

"We do." Charli looked over his shoulder into the hallway. "Can we step inside?"

"Absolutely. Make yourselves comfortable."

Montgomery rushed over to the living room, sitting on a chocolate brown leather couch. There was a matching loveseat to the right, which Matthew and Charli chose.

"Mr. Mowery, we have received more definitive findings from the medical examiner's office. They discovered Bryce was hit on the head shortly before he died, and he also suffered from a broken wrist that wasn't consistent with a normal fall. Additionally, the rope used to hang him does not contain any of Bryce's DNA aside from where the noose made contact with his throat, though it does contain the DNA of another individual. For those reasons, his death has been ruled a homicide."

"Yes!" Montgomery jumped out of his seat, pointing at Matthew and Charli as if he'd just won a horse racing bet. "I knew it! I knew Bryce didn't kill himself!"

Charli breathed a sigh of relief at his enthusiastic reaction, but it left as quickly as it'd come. Soon, the realization sank in, and Montgomery's eyes grew empty as he thought about what this really meant.

His son hadn't wanted to die. It hadn't been his choice, and his last moments were spent in terror and agony. Montgomery's shoulders fell, and his entire body deflated as he practically melted back into the couch.

"I'm very sorry. I can't fathom the grief you feel." Actually, Charli could, but this wasn't the time to tell a grieving parent about her own past.

"I already knew. I always knew. I don't know why it's so difficult to hear." Montgomery shook his head, his expression dazed. "Do you know who did this?"

Charli met the man's gaze, knowing she was about to

bring Montgomery even more grief. "We don't have any obvious suspects at the moment."

Montgomery swallowed hard. There was no more joy. Just the emptiness of knowing someone ended his boy's life, and he was helpless to do anything about it.

"My son made a lot of mistakes, but he wasn't a bad person. He didn't deserve this. You have to find who killed him."

Matthew leaned forward, his hands resting on his knees. "Sir, we'll do absolutely everything we can to discover who is responsible, and maybe you can help with that."

"How?" Montgomery's word was pleading.

"I know you said you didn't know anyone who would want to harm Bryce, and to say someone wanted to harm your son sounds extreme. Perhaps think of it in less severe terms. Do you know anyone who disliked him?" Charli softened her expression when Montgomery made eye contact.

Montgomery let out a dry chuckle. "Of course, many people disliked Bryce. He could get an attitude quick when he wasn't getting his way, even with me. I guess I spoiled him too much or something. Hell, maybe I spoiled him to death." Montgomery's breath caught on the last word, and he closed his eyes.

Charli waited until he'd composed himself. "We're not saying that's what happened. We only want to explore all avenues."

"Detective, I promise, if I had an avenue for you, I would've told you when we first spoke. I want nothing more than to find out what monster did this."

Charli nodded in understanding. "Are you familiar with Aaron Eldridge?"

Montgomery frowned. "Yes, why?"

Matthew adjusted on the loveseat. "He recently sold a valuable strip of riverfront property. From what we've learned, he and Bryce hung out at bars sometimes, according to local sources."

"Right, right, I remember that." Montgomery stroked his chin, which looked to be in need of a shave. "Didn't know the kid very well and didn't know he spent a lot of time with Bryce, but I'm not surprised. Bryce always found his way to other wealthy friends, like Roland. He surrounded himself with people of a certain...caliber, even those with new money."

Charli did her best not to turn her nose up at this. Montgomery was trying to be diplomatic in his wording, but the notion that low-income earners weren't worth hanging around was abhorrent. It wouldn't help her with this case to analyze Montgomery's moral failings, however.

Matthew asked Montgomery about his knowledge of Blair and Tanya. He was familiar with the former but said he knew very little about the latter. "Bryce wasn't a bad man, but my boy liked his women. Blair knew that about him from the get-go and seemed perfectly fine with the situation."

"Mr. Mowery, we asked if you could think of anyone who would want to hurt Bryce." Charli braced herself. "Is there anyone who might want to hurt you by hurting Bryce? An enemy who might be eager to get revenge in such a way?"

Mowery stared at her for so long that Charli thought he wouldn't answer. She let the silence rest, knowing most people couldn't resist filling it. After what felt like hours, Mowery ran a hand down his face. "A person doesn't get to my level of success without making an enemy or two."

"Anyone specific you can name?"

His face was pale. "I've knocked heads with every developer in this area. Wrestled with bank execs, realty agents." He shook his head. "I guess my list would be pretty long."

She gentled her voice. "Would you start making that list

for us? Then sort them based on how dangerous you think they could possibly be?"

As though it was an agonizing process, Mowery nodded. "Yeah, I'll do that."

Charli understood. How terrible would it be to know that you were responsible for the death of your child?

She changed the subject. "How much time did Bryce spend working for your company?"

Montgomery snorted. "Like I told you before, Bryce didn't work. Even as a boy, he hated going to work with me. He didn't have an office. Didn't get a paycheck. I don't know why you can't get that through your head."

"But—"

Montgomery glanced at his watch. "I've got to go. I have an appointment and can't be late."

Charli was tempted to ask him what was more important than helping them find the person who murdered his son but managed to keep the question behind her teeth. "Of course. If you think of anything—"

"I know, I know...I'll call."

On the way to the car, Matthew shifted his hands into his pockets and stared up at the sparse clouds above.

"What?" Charli eyed him.

"Do you think there's anything suspicious about Montgomery Mowery?"

Aside from him being a snobby asshole?

She shrugged. "What do you think of him?"

"It just feels like he's withholding information. If what Tanya Greenwood said is correct, then Bryce was working for the development business and Montgomery is lying about it."

But Charli didn't believe that was true. "Tanya told me specifically that Bryce didn't want to tell anyone. I don't think Montgomery knew. And as for the other details of

Bryce's life, I doubt Montgomery and Bryce were close enough for his father to know anything."

Matthew shrugged. "We can't rule him out as a suspect. You know that a family member is most often the perpetrator in a homicide."

Of course Charli knew this. She knew every annual statistic that the Federal Bureau of Investigation dispersed. And it wasn't lost on Charli that their most recent investigation was an uncharacteristic serial murderer. Those kinds of cases were exceedingly rare. What were the odds that her next case was also homicide by a stranger?

But Montgomery being innocent didn't mean this was a random murder. There were plenty of other people Bryce could've pissed off.

"I'm not writing him off, obviously, but I saw him at the crime scene. You didn't. He seemed to be genuinely grieving."

"Looks can be deceiving."

Charli flashed Matthew a sideways look but decided against telling Matthew how insulting his comment was. She was a damned good detective and great at reading a potential suspect.

"Like I said, I'm open to all possibilities, but right now, there is one possibility we haven't explored."

"You've got Aaron Eldridge's address?"

"Right here." Charli held up her notebook. She was about to suggest they head over there when her phone rang.

Matthew looked down at the random number on the screen. "Who is it?"

"No clue." Charli lifted the phone to her ear. "Hello?"

"I need help, right now. You need to come to me ASAP."

Charli couldn't place the desperate voice. It was a woman, that much was clear, but the tone was so high-pitched from panic that she couldn't identify it.

"I'm sorry, who—"

"I'm at Cork n' Brew Pub." The voice was even more urgent now. "Come now! I've got information about Bryce."

Charli firmed up her voice. "Who is this?"

"It's Blair. Blair Daughtry." Within the unease was a hint of annoyance, as if Charli should already know.

But Charli had never heard the young woman sound like this. Lounging by the pool, learning about Bryce's death, she'd been calm and ambivalent. Her apathy had created a coolness to her tone that wasn't present now.

Which begged the question, why was she so freaked out? What information could she have obtained that would send her into a panic attack? She'd barely cared about the news of Bryce's suicide, and now this?

"What have you learned?" Charli didn't want to wait until they arrived at the bar to learn more.

But she had to because Blair wasn't budging. "No, come to the pub. I don't want to talk over the phone. I don't know if someone could be listening to my phone…" The woman let out a long, shaky breath. "God, I can't believe I'm caught up in this."

"I'll be there soon." Charli hung up and turned to find a confused Matthew staring at her.

"What the hell was that all about?"

"Contact Janice. Tell her we got a tip about Bryce, and we'll be at Cork n' Brew Pub speaking to Blair Daughtry. I want someone at the precinct to know where we are and why we're there."

Matthew's brow furrowed. "Is that necessary?"

Was it? The creeping sensation of dread crawling up her spine was her answer.

"Yes. Whatever Blair has just learned, she doesn't feel safe sharing the information."

18

B lair Daughtry slammed an empty shot glass down on the top of a back corner table. The lighting was dim this far back in the bar from where a bulb had gone out in the lamp hanging over her head. But even in the dim lighting, her puffy eyes were visible to Charli. She swiped at them with her hands as the detectives approached.

"Who is this?" Blair's eyes darted toward Matthew, and Charli could read the distrust in her gaze.

"This is my partner, Detective Church. He's working Bryce's case with me."

"Okay, I guess." Blair leaned back in her chair, her movements slow and shaky. The pungent scent of her breath insinuated that the shot she just took hadn't been her only drink.

After grabbing the two seats across from Blair, Charli leaned forward, keeping her voice low. "What's going on?"

Blair drew in a shaky breath. "Something strange happened earlier today. I was at Olive's," she gestured to the glass, "drinking my sorrows away, I guess some people might say."

Did the girl care more for Bryce than she'd let on? And if she'd been at the ritzy bar before, why move to this less than stellar place? And had she driven?

Charli held in the questions she wanted to pepper at the woman and forced her face into the most sympathetic expression she could muster. "Losing a friend is hard, and I'm so sorry you're going through this."

Tears welled in the young woman's eyes, but she swiped them away. "That's not even why I'm crying." Blair covered her face with her hands, and Charli exchanged a confused glance with Matthew while they waited for her to compose herself.

Charli pushed a glass of water toward the girl. "Drink some of this."

Blair gulped greedily, then grimaced and stuck out her tongue as if she'd tasted something bad. She took another drink, though, and seemed a bit steadier when she set the glass back down. "Sorry. I'm just…" She shrugged.

"Scared?" Charli offered.

Tears welled again, but the young woman blinked them away. "Yes."

"What are you afraid of?"

Blair gazed at Charli for a long moment before blurting, "A man I kind of know was at Olive's, and he was dog drunk, and I think he recognized me because he'd seen me out with Bryce, so he came over and bought me some drinks and then started saying some really weird things."

Charli held up a hand to slow Blair down. She pushed the water back into the girl's hands. "Who was this man?"

Blair gulped another couple swallows. "Jack Derringer. He's an older guy. I guess he is on some kind of construction planning committee. Honestly, I don't understand what the hell he does, but he was at these parties thrown by big development people in Savannah. I barely even met him. I think

Bryce introduced us once. Like I said, he saw me at the bar and offered to buy me a drink, so I talked to him."

Matthew frowned. "So, some random guy offers to buy you a drink, you barely know him, and you agree to stay there and talk to him? Why would you do—"

Charli kicked him under the table, cutting him off. She knew he must be thinking about his estranged daughter, but geesh, lecturing a witness during the middle of an interview? She kicked him again just to make sure he got the message.

By the look he shot her, he'd gotten it loud and clear.

Blair scoffed. "Why am I the one being questioned here? I called you! But for your information, this kind of thing happens to me all the time." She tossed a strand of maroon hair over her shoulder. "A lot of older men are interested in me, especially after seeing me around town with Bryce. I figured, hey, I'd get free drinks, and if we hit it off, maybe a shopping trip. My parents have taken away all my cards after I maxed them out, and I've been bored out of my mind."

This time, it was their witness Charli wanted to kick, and she curled her feet around the base of her chair to keep them from lashing out on their own accord.

"Perfectly understandable." Charli feigned polite understanding, though she didn't understand this girl and her thinking at all. "What happened after he bought you the drink?"

Blair rolled her eyes. "First, I found out he definitely didn't want to take me to dinner and shopping. I think he's gay, but whatever."

Charli curled her feet tighter around the chair legs. "What else did he tell you?"

"He was really drunk and started rambling about how he didn't think Bryce killed himself, and then he said he knew who might have done it."

This got Charli's full attention. She wanted to ask for a

name immediately but knew better than to force the conversation. It was better to let the witness share everything at their own pace.

"From what I was able to gather, Jack said that he'd been sort of mentoring Bryce and the two were working together when Aaron sold his riverfront property."

Charli needed to interrupt this time. She needed to make sure she got all the names down correctly. "Aaron who?"

"Aaron Eldridge. Apparently, Bryce had this whole big plan to turn Aaron's land into an open-air mall by the water, like they've got down by Myrtle Beach in South Carolina." Excitement broke through the tears from a moment ago. "Have you ever been to that mall? Oh my god, it's to die for." For the first time since their arrival, Blair's mouth formed into a bright smile.

Charli knew this would trigger Matthew, and sure enough, his face distorted in disgust. Charli shared the sentiment. How could a person be so vapid that she smiled over memories of a mall while discussing her lover's death? And, once again, Charli had no idea why Blair had appeared to be so upset when she clearly didn't care about Bryce's passing.

She was more eager than ever to find out...if Blair would get to the damn point.

Matthew drummed his fingers on the table. "Focus, can we?"

Blair scowled at him. "This is all important information, okay?" She tossed her hair back again. "Anyway, Jack said it was an amazing idea. His committee loved it, but they turned Bryce down. Bryce couldn't understand why, so he kept bugging Jack about it. Jack finally told him the committee had learned that it was useless to make a bid because it was already going to Chester Crabtree."

Charli perked up in her chair. "Chester Crabtree. As in Crabtree Industries?"

"Yeah, they're apparently, like, a really big deal. Jack told me they're the second biggest development business in Savannah, after Montgomery Mowery's firm. I do know about Chester, though, and what I know is nothing good."

"I don't understand." Matthew looked as confused as Charli felt. "If Crabtree's business is second to the Mowerys', why wouldn't Bryce have a chance with the bid? His father's business is larger, more established. Wouldn't they have the money for it?"

"That's the thing. It wasn't just about that. He told me Chester Crabtree is a shady dude, and I don't disagree. He was bribing a lot of people for that land, especially Aaron Eldridge. Which, let's be real, Bryce could've bribed him too, but Chester had blackmail on many of the committee members that no money could compete with. Jack said Bryce got really mad about it right after Jack explained everything. He called Aaron right away. They fought over the phone, and then set up a meeting with Bryce, Aaron, and Chester. There was also something about salamanders or maybe snakes. Like I said, he was drunk."

Charli thumbed through her notebook. "What happened at the meeting?"

"Jack doesn't know. He wasn't there, but he thinks it went badly. And he thinks it's really weird that a week after that meeting, Bryce killed himself. He didn't straight up say it, but I'm positive he thinks Chester was involved."

Something still wasn't adding up. The dead light above Blair flickered, exposing small streaks of mascara down her cheeks.

Charli eyed her before the light went dim again. "Blair, I don't understand. Why has this got you so devastated? Are you upset because you don't think Bryce killed himself now? If I remember correctly, you never thought he committed suicide to begin with."

Blair scoffed, like the answer should've been obvious. "I'm upset because, now, I know about all the stuff that's been going on. I didn't wanna hear this. That asshole Jack just put me on Chester's kill list."

Charli and Matthew shared a look. They didn't have to say it, but they both thought Blair was jumping to conclusions and severely overreacting.

Blair tossed her arms up in the air. "Fine, don't believe me, but I know about Chester. I've had girlfriends who've spent time at his mansion, who used to hook up with him. And I've told myself for years that I'd never accept a date from that man. He could offer to take me to Europe for a month, and I still wouldn't go."

This softened Charli a bit. Although Blair Daughtry certainly was a drama queen in general, Charli trusted a woman's intuition when it came to dangerous men. Even women as narcissistic as Blair could have good instincts for safety. This was the only type of intuition that Charli fully believed because she'd felt a shudder of it herself that day Madeline was taken. Gut instincts could usually be ignored until they were about safety.

Charli didn't have to fake compassion this time. "What stories had you heard?"

"He's incredibly abusive. I've seen my friends with bruises on their arms and chest after some of his yacht parties. One of my girlfriends, Anna, said he threatened to kill her because she talked to another guy during one of his events, and they'd only been dating for a couple of weeks. If he's going to threaten to kill her over that, why wouldn't he kill me for talking to you about this?"

"We don't even know if Crabtree is involved in Bryce's death." Matthew tapped his finger against the dark grain of the wood table. "I think it's a little preemptive for you to be afraid of him."

This actually seemed to calm Blair a little. "You're right. I mean, you guys still believe he killed himself, right? So maybe there's nothing to worry about?" Charli and Matthew didn't answer, just looked on quietly for a moment. It was all Blair needed to see to understand. She thumped her fists onto the table, making the glasses jump. "Oh, dammit. So, he *was* murdered? And it was Chester!"

Charli held up a hand. "We didn't say—"

"I need police assistance!" Her voice ratcheted up several octaves. "You guys have to watch over me! I will not die because of that asshole! Dammit, why did Jack ever tell me about this?" Blair started to hyperventilate as panic overtook her. She gripped the table corners as she gasped.

Despite Matthew's reservations about their witness, he reached out and put his hand on hers. "Blair, relax. You need to focus on catching your breath. Breathe in and out slowly. You can do it."

Blair kept her eyes locked on Matthew and did as he said, forcing slow breaths that would calm her nervous system. Once she was breathing more normally, Charli tried to reason with her.

"Blair, we don't know that Crabtree was involved, and even if he is, there is no way that he knows Jack talked to you. We don't have any reason right now to give you a constant police escort."

"But I—"

"I've been to your home. I think it's reasonable for me to assume you have a security system?" Charli paused until Blair nodded. "And I'm guessing that your mom's home most of the time. She doesn't work out of the house?"

"No, she doesn't."

"Okay. What we can do is drive you back home, and until we solve this mystery, I suggest you lie low for a while. You'll be secure at your house."

Charli doubted Blair would much enjoy being stuck at home, but she was fairly safe there. Charli had seen some of the state-of-the-art security systems rich people could buy nowadays. Chester Crabtree, being as wealthy as he was, would know about them too and would think twice before trying to break in.

"Okay, fine, but I need another drink first." Blair got out of her chair and walked over to the bar, giving Matthew and Charli a minute alone.

Matthew scowled at her retreating back. "How far is her house?"

"It's in the Historic District, close to mine."

Matthew groaned. "That's twenty minutes away. I don't know if I can handle her for twenty more minutes."

Charli laughed. "You'll survive. On the way, shoot a message to Janice and ask her to collect information on Jack Derringer."

"What about Aaron Eldridge?"

"Have her start digging things up on him after Derringer. Seems like Jack wants to share what he knows, and we should make ourselves available."

As far as Charli knew, all Eldridge did was sell a strip of land. But Jack Derringer had reason to suspect foul play, and hopefully, he had even more information than he shared with Blair.

What else would he be able to share about Chester Crabtree? Before they spoke with Crabtree themselves, Charli wanted all the information she could gather on him. The more dirt they had, the more likely they'd be able to back Crabtree into a corner and catch him in a lie.

19

His feet pushed against the dark hardwood floor, rolling his chair back toward the open window. A hand with ruby red nail polish reached up and fiddled with his zipper, pulling it back up into position. There was just enough room for the woman to crawl out from under his desk.

"How was that?" She smiled up at him.

"Oh, honey, you know that nobody does it like you," Chester answered through heavy breaths.

And he meant it. He had a lot of women at his disposal. Some would even say an endless number, but this sweet thing was by far his favorite lately. She did things to his body that no one else had been able to.

Chester didn't know why she was so much hotter than the usual broads he kept around. Perhaps it was her lower class. Usually, Chester made it a rule to hang out with wealthy women. For years, he'd been telling himself that rich women wouldn't bother him about his money, since they had their own.

That ended up not being true. The women from wealthy

families still wanted expensive trips, gifts, endless fine dining. When Chester figured out that there was no woman on Earth who'd see him as anything but a bag of cash, he'd decided that he might as well date broke women since they appreciated anything he did for them.

His new plan was working out in his favor.

First, because she was extraordinarily eager to please him, she didn't want to lose her place in his life. And second, she wasn't used to having money, so she had lower expectations than upper-class ladies did. Chester ended up spending significantly less money on her than he had on any of his other tramps.

"Why don't you go get cleaned up in my bathroom? I made reservations for dinner."

Her eyes widened. "Reservations? Chester, you know I can't be seen with you right now. All the rich diners around here will recognize me."

"Relax, sweetheart. You think I'm an imbecile? I didn't make reservations in Savannah. We'll be taking a limo to Beaufort."

"We're going to South Carolina? Oh." A smile brightened her pretty features. "Well, thank you. That's awful sweet. What's the occasion?"

"Thought you could use a pick-me-up after the news of Bryce's death."

She poked him in the chest, a playful expression on her face. "Are you kidding me? The news was the pick-me-up. I've never been so relieved."

Hips swinging, she sashayed to the bathroom off Chester's grandiose office. He spent so much time in this building, he'd made certain it had been built to his exact specifications. A dazzling chandelier hung over his office desk. White wainscoting surrounded him on the walls, leading down to the marble tile floor. The real masterpiece was the bathroom, though. He'd wanted a full bath with a jetted tub connected to his office.

Most would consider that a little much, but Chester viewed it as a necessary expense. He couldn't get through a workday without a woman paying him a sensual visit. He needed a romantic place to seduce them, and the tub was perfect for his purposes. That is, when they got bored of the full-size bed in the attached room.

He could live here if he wanted to, which he sometimes did.

While she readied herself, Chester went back to what he'd been doing prior to her pleasant distraction. The plans for Bryce's open-air mall were before him, and he was studying them once more for any potential flaws.

There were none, though. Chester hated to admit that the little asshole had done something right, but he had. This idea was genius. With the nearby hotels, this mall was going to rake in money from both locals and tourists visiting Savannah. All shops would be high-end, sucking as much cash from customers as possible.

And Chester would get it all.

It was Chester's path to finally burying Montgomery Mowery's company and becoming the biggest development agency in the state. Okay, maybe burying was a little dramatic. Montgomery still had plenty of other avenues to make his income, but he was no longer going to be the richest man in Savannah's development game. Chester would soon rise to the top.

How ironic that it was Montgomery's boy who'd helped him do it, though his old man would never know that his playboy son actually had a brain in his head. Bless Bryce for being so secretive about his plans. There was only a small circle of people who knew this was originally Bryce's idea, and none of them were stupid enough to fuck with Chester.

He rose from his chair, walking over to the bathroom to knock on the door. "How long until you're ready?"

"Uh, I need to take a shower, so half an hour or so? Why?"

"I'm out of cigars, and I want one for the road."

"So? Have your assistant get one."

"She's already left for the evening. I let her out early when I knew you were coming, so we'd have some privacy."

Actually, Chester couldn't care less about keeping their sexual encounters private. Everyone knew what he did while at work. But it just so happened that he'd done the same thing with his new secretary recently, and then found out later she was the jealous type. He didn't want her to hear them and then start a catfight.

He'd have to fire her, of course, because he couldn't have his secretary leaving early every single time he wanted to screw someone in his office. But until he got a replacement, he had to run interference.

Speaking of firing, where the hell was his damn designer? He'd asked her to review the damn riverfront plans today, and she hadn't shown. So what if it was her day off? He paid the bitch enough. She'd better be at his beck and call.

"I'm just going to head out real quick. I'll be back in thirty. Be ready."

"Okay, see you soon!"

With the keys to his Mercedes in hand, Chester headed out to the parking garage. The garage was usually empty at this time, so Chester whipped around when he heard footsteps coming up behind him.

No one was there.

A chill went down Chester's spine. He scanned the area. Had he been hearing things? Had he heard the echo of steps from someone on the second level?

"Hello?"

Chester wasn't easily rattled. His presence in this town

was ominous, and people didn't screw with him. And yet, he couldn't shake the pit forming in his stomach. Something seemed wrong. Felt wrong.

When nothing but silence answered, Chester shook his head and turned toward the direction of his car. He needed to relax. Maybe Bryce's death had gotten to him more than he thought.

The guy was a prick. Chester didn't care about him personally, but it did make him feel a little less invincible. If harm could befall the Mowerys, one of the most prominent families in the city, could something happen to Chester too?

No use in obsessing about every footstep, though.

Chester swung his keys in a circle on his finger and began to whistle in an attempt to convince himself he wasn't worried. He'd only gotten in a few notes of "Sexual Healing" when a noise stopped him cold.

Maybe it was…hell, he couldn't even think of her name. But maybe she'd gotten ready faster than she thought she would and had run out to join him.

His gut told him otherwise. So did his heart.

It was pounding and his legs felt weak as he spun around.

Relief washed over him when recognition hit.

"Oh, man, you scared me!" His chuckle came out half hysterical. "I thought I was being followed or some shit. Guess this whole Bryce thing is making me a little para—"

A fist punched him in his stomach, knocking the air out of his lungs.

Shocked at the suddenness of the attack, he stared at the hand still pressed against his gut. It wasn't just a fist, though. As the hand retreated, a silver blade dripping with blood was revealed.

His blood.

Words couldn't form on his lips. He could only hold out his bloodied hand, mouth ajar, and stare at the man who had done this to him. Chester made no move to flee. That would have required a level of intellectual processing that he wasn't capable of at the moment. Perhaps if he'd been given another minute, he would've understood the situation well enough to run away.

He wasn't given another minute, though. The knife was thrust forward again, this time stabbing between his ribs. There was a sucking sound as it was yanked out, but Chester only heard the pounding of his heart in his ears.

Chester tried to talk, tried to scream, especially when pain overrode the shock and sent him to his knees. Pain radiated from every inch of his torso, and it became harder to breathe. He tried to stand, but his legs wouldn't move, and he fell over onto his side.

Why?

The question echoed through his mind as he attempted to understand what was happening to him. Panic like he'd never known followed as the breath he attempted to take didn't deliver the oxygen he so desperately needed.

A wave of iron flooded his tongue, and when he coughed, a spray of it shot out on the concrete, just like he'd seen in movies. But this wasn't a movie.

This was real. He was dying.

And the person who'd killed him was just standing there, smiling down on him almost benevolently.

"Why?"

This time the word did come, though it was barely above a whisper.

The last thing Chester saw was his attacker's shrug.

20

The chest that had been rising and falling only seconds ago came to a stop. Glassy eyes stared at me, the life draining from them as I watched. There was still pink in his cheeks, and he hadn't turned blue the way Bryce had, but I knew he was gone.

My hard-on was still on high alert, though. I had no idea the power of taking a life could be so thrilling. So intimate. So damn sexual.

I wasn't so far gone that I didn't realize that was a problem.

This entire adventure was only supposed to be a means to an end. Killing Chester started with one purpose...to further my own success. But what a joy it was to plunge my knife into flesh and watch life slip away, knowing this human being would never live another day.

Because of me.

Because of my hands. My decisions. My power over them.

The first man I killed had been out of necessity, and I hadn't even known the guy, so it had been easy to detach myself from the entire situation. Bryce, though, had been different. I'd known him, and his death had hit me hard.

There would be no puking once I got home, not this time. I didn't feel the same horror I had when I watched Bryce swinging from the rafters. It was already so easy. Was it supposed to become this easy so quickly?

I leaned down over what once had been Chester Crabtree and prowled through his pockets, but as the blood pooled around him, I took a step back. I needed to be careful.

Blood was spattered on my jacket, but I'd worn a rain-proof one for this very reason. I'd thought of everything.

There'd be no bloody footprints, no fingerprints because of the now bloody gloves on my hands. All I needed to do was walk away, and they'd have nothing but the size of the blade as evidence. I knew where all the cameras in the parking garage were and had disabled the one that would cause me the most trouble.

My planning had been nearly perfect.

I wasn't ready to walk away, not yet. I wished to freeze this moment in time forever. I was tempted to pull out my phone and take a picture, a memento. But I couldn't have something like that on my phone or computer. No, I'd have to settle for my mental imagery, which meant I was going to stare at Chester as long as I could before making my exit.

The size of the pool of blood around his body came as a surprise. I'd never really thought about how much blood the human body held. The blue veins that poked out of my pale skin seemed so small. How were they able to hold so much liquid?

His face grew whiter as it flowed out of him. I could've stared at it all night, watching his body stiffen, but my moment of joy was interrupted by the clicking of heels.

Shit.

This wasn't in the plan. Everyone was supposed to already be gone.

I'd even slipped a little ipecac syrup into the pretty little security guard's drink earlier. I'd thought of everything, and it pissed me off that someone would dare screw it up.

Slipping behind one of the enormous columns, I held my breath and listened intently, gripping the knife close to my chest.

"Chester?" It was a woman's voice, soft but high-pitched. "Are you out here?"

The sound caused a tingle to shoot up my spine. What would it sound like if I squeezed that throat? How loud could that gentle voice scream?

I closed my eyes as I pictured the heels that were getting increasingly nearer. Were they a shiny red pleather? How tall did they make her stand? Would she accidentally kick them off as she writhed under me?

Chester hadn't been enough. I knew that now.

How would it feel to watch a woman waste away under my grasp? And what better opportunity than this moment, when I had already created a crime scene?

Pulling the gun from my pocket, ideas flashed through my mind. Maybe I could set the scene up to look like a murder-suicide.

It would be so perfect.

The heels grew closer…closer still.

"Where are you?"

I nearly jumped when she yelled but managed to hold myself perfectly still.

"Asshole." Her voice was even louder this time. "Where the hell is he?"

I waited for her to scream bloody murder the moment she discovered the corpse I'd left behind. To my surprise, no scream came. Instead, she muttered something I couldn't understand and her clicking started again, this time in the other direction.

She hadn't seen the body on the driver's side of the car. All she'd needed to do was walk around the front of the vehicle to get that surprise, but instead, she was walking away.

Slowly, I inched from behind the column and found that the woman had stopped about halfway down the parking garage. She was fidgeting with her purse.

How reckless of her not to have her keys ready to go. Didn't she know how vulnerable she was in a place like this?

I inched along the concrete wall. If I moved quickly, it wouldn't be too late to take her. As I creeped in the shadows, I kept my eyes glued to her.

She had short black hair that fell just above her shoulders in tight curls. The heels were tan but not too tall. It wouldn't hurt too bad if she kicked one of them into me during the scuffle. She was probably in her late thirties, and quite a sight to see. I couldn't see her face, but I could imagine mascara-laden eyes staring up at me as I slowly choked her to death.

My pants tightened at the crotch at the thought.

She finally wrestled her keys out of her purse, and I moved closer. Would I have time to pull off her clothes and sink into her body as she breathed her last breath?

No.

This needed to look like a murder-suicide, I reminded myself, and processed through the steps I'd need to take to create a convincing scene. As long as she didn't lock the door, I'd be able to pull her out of her vehicle and drag her over to Chester's body without much trouble. Any bruises I might leave on her creamy skin would be ones the police would think were created during her struggle with the man they'd think she killed.

So perfect.

She sank into the car but didn't pull the door closed. Instead, her foot dangled out.

I nearly laughed at how easy this was going to be.

I was at the car right behind her when she pulled out her phone and started to type. Even better, she'd be distracted when I made my move. Then...she lifted the phone to her ear.

Shit.

Moving back into the shadows, I waited to see what happened next. I leaned against a black SUV near her car, lying in wait.

Surprise stabbed through me when another phone began to ring from the other side of the parking garage. Dammit, it belonged to Crabtree. Wait, was this woman trying to call the man I'd just killed?

The first ring stopped just as her car door closed and the engine burned to life. The sequence of events told a story of their own.

Who was the woman, though?

After she'd driven away, I headed back to Chester's corpse and searched for his phone. It was locked, of course, but the notification on the screen shared the recent missed call from a Tanya Greenwood.

What the hell?

One of Chester's hands was covered in gore, but the other was stretched above his head. Being careful of the blood, I moved the phone to his thumb, hoping his fingertip was still warm enough to register the print. It was, and his phone unlocked for me.

Tapping Tanya's name took me to a long string of text messages. At first, I'd only planned to kill the woman in the garage for the thrill of it. It would have simply been a crime of passion with the added benefit that would have also helped me cover my tracks.

Until now.

Reading over the series of texts, I realized I had a more pressing reason to murder the woman who'd just called him.

She'd betrayed me.

Deceived me.

Burning with anger, I took Chester's watch, wallet, and keys, wanting this to look like a robbery gone bad. Slipping the bloody jacket off, I stuffed them into the bag I'd carried in with me. I also exchanged the bloody gloves for clean ones. Pulling a new hoodie over my head, I lifted the hood up until my face was in its shadows.

Slipping behind the wheel of Chester's car, I started the purring engine. Too bad I wasn't going to keep this beauty. Instead, I was going to drive to the bad part of town and leave it, engine running. I doubted it would take more than an hour before some chop shop had rendered it nearly unrecognizable.

As I drove, I stewed over everything I'd learned.

Besides deceiving me, what else had Tanya done?

I needed to find out.

21

Matthew stepped through his front door, dodging the pile of boxes that sat in the entryway. They were left over from his move, containing the things he hadn't bothered to unpack, even though he'd lived in this place for almost a year now.

It still didn't feel like his home, and maybe it never would if he didn't get the heap of cardboard out of the way. But it was difficult to make all his belongings, which once existed in a three-bedroom home, fit into this much smaller space.

It wasn't as if he had the time to finish unpacking anyway, he was always so busy. Okay, admittedly, he could have found more time, but he couldn't muster the willpower to get cleaning.

He slammed the door behind him, the noise echoing against the hardwood floor of his living room. His stomach grumbled, and he prayed there was something in the kitchen for him to eat. Charli had just dropped him off, and because she was driving, he didn't think to ask her to stop for some takeout, which was what he usually did for dinner.

There was a pack of ramen in his pantry, the kind in a

cup that he could pop straight into the microwave. Perfect. He wouldn't have to wash a bowl after he was done eating. He only had a fork to contend with. After unwrapping the fitted plastic, he turned on the sink and filled the cup up to the designated waterline before placing it in the microwave for two minutes.

Matthew knew you weren't actually supposed to microwave these things, something about the foam container causing cancer, but whatever. Everyone did it anyway, right? Who took the time to boil water, put it in the container, and then wait three minutes for the noodles to soften? Not Matthew, that was for sure.

When the microwave rang out to confirm it had finished, Matthew walked his meal over to the small round dining table sitting not far from his fridge. It was pathetically tiny compared to the formal dining table he had before his divorce. The old table had hosted many Thanksgiving dinners, though Matthew didn't make it to all of them due to work emergencies. He'd never be able to fit a turkey on this flimsy dollar store nightmare.

And as if it wasn't crowded enough, a thousand-piece jigsaw that was only a quarter completed was splayed out on top of it. Matthew started it a month ago, and though he had no intention of finishing it any time soon, he couldn't bring himself to put it away. For the most part, he ignored it and ate out on the couch watching television. But tonight, his dinner would have to share a place with the puzzle because he wouldn't be watching TV while he ate.

He was too consumed with the case. They had several leads on Bryce Mowery's case, but no answers. They hadn't been able to get ahold of Jack Derringer. He wasn't home or answering his phone.

Blair Daughtry seemed convinced that Chester Crabtree was somehow involved, but that didn't mean much. She was obviously terrified of the guy. Matthew didn't question that the man was an abusive asshole, but an abusive asshole didn't necessarily equate to murderer.

After failing to get in touch with Jack Derringer, Charli and Matthew attempted to find Crabtree. He also wasn't home, and his office was closed, according to the business hours listed outside the entrance.

That was why Charli dropped Matthew off. They were both resigned to the fact they'd have to wait until tomorrow to conduct more interviews.

Truth be told, Matthew still had a weird feeling about Montgomery Mowery. Charli didn't seem to share it, but how often did homicide lead to a family member? Most of the time. That was how often.

Plus, the information Montgomery had shared didn't add up. He'd said that Bryce wasn't involved in the business, didn't have the desire to work, while they now had the knowledge that Bryce did have aspirations within his father's business.

Maybe that had pissed Montgomery off. Perhaps he didn't want his son competing with him for control of the enterprise. People had murdered over less.

Matthew looped some ramen around his fork and lifted it to his mouth, nearly burning his lips off in the process. Nights like these really made him miss his wife's cooking. Sure, they'd grown apart and she'd ended up cheating on him, but she was an amazing cook. When he lived with her, she'd have pasta, meatloaf, and any number of dishes ready when he got home.

He wondered what she and Chelsea were having for dinner tonight on the other side of the country. The thought put a foul taste in his mouth, one that the saltiness of the ramen couldn't drown out. More than his ex-wife's cooking, he missed his little girl. He'd tried calling her since he returned to Savannah, but she hadn't answered or returned the call.

Chelsea, who used to run to him every time he came home from work, no longer wanted to speak to him at all. It would've been easy to accuse his wife of poisoning her against him, and in Matthew's weakest moments, he often did. But Judy wasn't solely at fault. Maybe if Matthew had prioritized his family over his job, Chelsea wouldn't be ignoring him now.

Matthew willed himself to focus on the details of the case, but it was hard to do with his family on his mind. Ever since his failed trip out West, the memories of them flooded back whenever he was in this mess of an apartment.

He was about to call Chelsea again when Charli's name popped up on the screen and the phone buzzed in his hand. A small smile crossed Matthew's lips. He could use a friendly chat about now.

Yeah, right.

This wouldn't be a leisurely call, he knew. They'd just been in the car together less than fifteen minutes ago, and Charli wouldn't call him to talk so soon, surely. This was certainly about the investigation.

"What's the latest?" Matthew scooped another forkful of noodles into his mouth, eating quickly in case he had to leave.

Charli let out a long breath. "Well, we can cross Crabtree off our list of suspects."

"That was fast. You're certain it wasn't him?"

An even longer sigh this time. "Pretty sure."

"The guy must have a damn solid alibi for you to write him off so expeditiously."

"No, not quite. I didn't actually get to speak with the man."

Why was his partner acting so squirrely?

"How can you clear him if you didn't talk to him?" Matthew forked another bite while he waited for the normally articulate Charli Cross to share the information rattling around in her head.

"Because he's dead."

Matthew almost choked on his ramen. "Yep, that's a pretty good sign."

"I'll be there in five. Be ready."

C harli hadn't even had time to grab something to eat or take a shower when she had to run back out to pick Matthew up. On the way, they both ran through the possible scenarios.

Finding Chester's body didn't necessarily rule him out as a murderer since it was possible that someone was killing off successful development leaders in Savannah. First Bryce, now Crabtree—there was a pattern, though why Bryce instead of Montgomery if that was the case? Who would benefit from executing them both?

Matthew stepped over the caution tape while Charli raised it a few inches to walk underneath. Soames was already present with his team, taking notes as the forensic photographer snapped photographs of Chester's lifeless corpse. An undisturbed pool of blood formed around the man's body.

"Matthew, Charli, funny seeing you two here."

She gave the man a fond smile. "Were you expecting anyone else?"

"Actually, I was expecting a quiet evening at home, but

instead, I had an unscheduled date with Chester Crabtree here."

Charli stared down at the body. His light gray shirt was soaked with blood.

"He's been stabbed." It wasn't a question. Even through the gore, Charli spotted a couple tears in Chester's shirt.

"Twice, as far as I can see. We haven't yet shifted the body, so there is always the chance that there are more wounds in the back. It seems to be a head-on assault, though."

Matthew squatted closer to the victim. "Any defensive wounds?"

"His hands and upper arms are clear, so it doesn't appear that Chester fought back." Usually, in a knife fight, the victim had slashes on their extremities where they tried to block the blows.

Charli circled the body. "So, he wasn't expecting this. Whoever approached him, he had no reason to think they'd cause him harm."

Matthew followed her train of thought. "Either someone he knew or a bystander that didn't raise any red flags until the very moment before he was attacked."

Matthew stepped away from the body, looking up at the ceiling. "Have we reviewed footage of that security camera yet?"

"The private security here at the parking garage did. Said that one wasn't working, but another camera caught the plate number of a vehicle that left."

Matthew was already turning away. "I'll go check it out."

"Fantastic. Thanks, Matt."

While he gathered information, Charli continued to talk to Soames. "Have you found any identifying evidence yet?"

"Wallet is gone, so could be that robbery was the motive. We'll have to run prints on his body, see if he was grabbed anywhere, or if there is any blood that belongs to someone else. I doubt the latter, considering the lack of defensive wounds. I don't see how our victim could have harmed his assailant enough to get DNA evidence, but we'll check under his fingernails and in his mouth, hope for some skin cells."

Charli could tell from Soames's tone of voice, he wasn't hopeful.

"This is a much different scene than what we found with Mowery. Bryce's death was made to look like an accident in hopes that we wouldn't find anything. Why would that same killer commit such an obvious murder? We could be dealing with two different killers. Why not make it appear that Crabtree also killed himself?"

Matthew reappeared by her side. "Maybe he somehow heard through the grapevine the police are aware that Bryce's death was a homicide, so he didn't feel the need to go through the effort again. I'm sure Montgomery would've told several family friends the truth by now. Or maybe we're wrong and it's not the same killer."

"All real possibilities. What did you learn?"

Matthew glanced down at his notepad. "A car was captured leaving the garage, and the plate's already been ran. The owner is Monica Height."

"I know her."

Charli turned to find the fresh-faced security guard who'd spoken. He couldn't have been older than twenty-four. His bright apple cheeks showed an eagerness to help, but his eyes revealed how disturbed he was by the image before him.

Charli felt bad for the kid. She remembered the first time she saw a dead body. It was a shock, but at least she was expecting it. She couldn't imagine going in for a normal day as a private security guard and having to deal with something like this.

"Are you the one who found the body?"

"Yes, ma'am, I am. I'm Josh Peterson. I had just taken over the post for the guard before me."

Charli jotted the name in her notebook. "Who was the person on shift before you? And when did their shift end?"

"That would be Amanda Reber. Her shift ended at nine. She was supposed to check the perimeter of the garage before she left, but she was feeling pretty sick to her stomach and asked if I could do it instead. But she definitely isn't involved with this. She's a super sweet girl. I know she would've been freaking out if she saw this."

A little blush rose on Josh's cheeks. Whoever this Amanda girl was, it seemed Josh had a bit of a crush on her.

Matthew stepped forward to join in the line of questioning. "And how do you know Monica Height?"

"She's one of the employees at Chester's office. I don't know what she does specifically, but I've seen them walk out to their cars together often, blueprints in their hand. I've never actually talked to her because whenever I see her, she looks pretty stressed. Chester could be a…direct guy."

It was a polite way to say he was an asshole, but Josh had the grace not to speak ill of the dead.

"Can you get us a number?"

"Yes, ma'am. We keep a directory of all the employees at the offices attached to the garage. So, yeah, I can get you her address and number. The directory is in my office. Actually, I came out here to say you should probably stop by my office anyway. I think there's something you need to see."

Charli wasted no time. "Let's go."

The security office was really more of a closet on the first floor of the parking garage. There was just enough room for a desk with the computer that held the security camera feeds. One chair was tucked tightly into the desk, so Charli and Matthew had to stand awkwardly behind him. Charli's shoulder bumped into Matthew's, causing him to back up farther into the corner.

She gave him another poke for good measure. "You know, this would be easier if you weren't the size of the Jolly Green Giant."

Grinning, he stood to his full six-two height. "Are you talking about the guy on the green bean can? Please, he's an inch tall at most."

Charli chuckled to herself before gaining her composure. It wasn't unusual for Matthew and Charli to joke during an investigation. Most officers and detectives did as a coping mechanism of stress, but she knew that to a young security guard like Josh, their humor could come across as inappropriate and insensitive.

Josh didn't seem to be paying them any attention, though, as he clicked away at the keyboard. "The camera that should have been capturing the area where Mr. Crabtree was killed had been turned toward the ceiling, so we can't see anything that happened to him."

Matthew groaned and Charli wanted to cuss. Instead, she settled on, "That's unfortunate." She'd need to let the forensics team know to dust that camera for prints.

Josh nodded. "Yeah, very unfortunate. It went offline, so to say, a little after seven o'clock. Whoever did it must have come up from behind because no one is in sight when the angle shifts from the cars to the ceiling."

Their killer was organized, it seemed.

"Here." The security guard tapped the screen. "I saw something when I looked back at the footage, besides the fact that Mrs. Height was on her phone as she was leaving. It's just a blip. It's hard to catch, but...there! Did you see that?"

Matthew squinted while Charli leaned so close she was practically in the security guard's lap. "No, not really."

He rewound the footage. "Pay attention to the far-right wall, in between the gray sedan and black SUV."

It truly was just a blip, a shadow of a body moving quickly between the cars.

"Great catch, kid. You should consider a job in the force someday." Matthew patted him on the shoulder.

Josh practically beamed with pride. "I don't have any idea who it could be. But there's one more thing you need to see."

He tapped a few more keys, and new video appeared. "This is the same camera that caught Mrs. Height leaving. A few minutes after she departed..." He tapped the screen. "Here. This is a different car, a Mercedes, though I wasn't able to catch the plate from the angle. On another camera, though, I was able to catch the license plate."

Charli pursed her lips. "Crabtree's?"

Josh nodded. "Yes, ma'am."

Matthew and Charli exchanged a look. "So, the killer stole his car? We need to put out an APB for the make and plate."

Charli leaned even closer and peered at the screen. "He's wearing a hood. Dammit. All I can see is a little bit of his chin."

After they watched the car cruise all the way through the garage and then turn onto the street, Josh clicked the stop button. "I'll give you guys the rest of the footage from the other cameras, but I've been rewatching the feeds in here and I didn't see anything. Whoever this is, I think they have inside information on where all the cameras are located."

"Can you rewind it? I want to get a good look at the build. From first glance, looks to be a man around six feet." Matthew pointed at the screen. "And yes, we're going to need copies for our own team to go over."

They played it back again, and Charli agreed with Matthew. They were definitely looking for a tall, slender man. Charli got her pen ready again. "Besides the other guards who work here, would anyone else know what the cameras can catch?"

"Well, yeah. All the office executives with businesses that use the garage. The owners can all sign into the feed themselves. And I guess they'd also be able to show it to any employee they wanted to. The business park hires our security agency. They're our clients, so they have access to the feeds and all our reports. What they do with that information is up to them."

That was a pretty comprehensive list of people, but it was a place to start.

Charli addressed the security guard. "We're definitely going to need that directory."

Matthew's foot bounced up and down in anticipation. "Where exactly do you wanna start, Charli?"

Charli tapped her bottom lip with her pen. "We should definitely begin with the one other person we can identify in the building around the time of the murder. Monica Height."

23

By the looks of Monica Height's home, she was paid well at Crabtree Industries. Her house was just outside downtown with ivory columns adorning a wraparound porch.

Matthew whistled in appreciation. "So, guess we know why she dealt with Crabtree despite him being a nightmare of a boss."

"No kidding."

The white wood planks creaked underneath their feet as they approached the front door. When Charli's fingertips brushed the doorbell, the extravagant jingle reverberated into the porch outside. After a full minute, she rang it again.

"Coming!" A male voice rang out, clearly unhappy about visitors calling so late in the evening. "Who is it?"

Charli identified them both and held her badge up to the peephole for the man's inspection. "We have a few questions about an investigation we're working. May we come in?"

A balding, stout older man opened the door. "What's this about?"

"We're looking for Monica Height."

The man's frown deepened. "What could you need Monica for?"

"Did I hear my name?" Monica popped up behind him.

"Uh, these officers want to speak to you."

Monica had dark hair and appeared a good ten years younger than her husband. As Charli introduced them for a second time, the woman seemed as distraught as the man that the police had showed up to their house.

"What can I do for you?" Monica looked them up and down, wiping her hands on a fuzzy robe the color of baby carrots.

She seemed nervous, and sweat had appeared on the bald man's forehead.

"Sorry to interrupt your evening, but this will only take a few minutes. Can we come in?" Matthew didn't simply ask but pushed his way through the door. Charli was right on his heels.

Charli wasn't imagining it. There were definitely shifty eyes between the married couple. They weren't comfortable with two cops in their home.

Were they simply nervous around law enforcement officials, or did they have something to hide?

"Will you, uh, just pardon us for a moment?" Her smile wavered at the corners. "We need to make sure our kids head to their rooms since it's so late."

Matthew nodded toward the stairs. "No problem."

Charli and Matthew waited briefly as two teenagers, a boy and a girl, exited the back of the house and went upstairs without so much as glancing at the detectives. A brunette ponytail bobbed along as the daughter rushed in front of her brother to get out of the way.

Charli expected that Monica and her husband would exit the living room soon after. But after another minute, there was still no sight of them.

Matthew looked down at Charli. "Perhaps we should see if everything is all right."

His tone was casual, but the implication was clear because he'd read her mind too. Matthew thought that, if they sneaked up on the couple, they might find out important information.

Charli was down with that.

"I'm on it." Charli kept her tread light, hoping not to be heard as she moved down the hall.

At the doorway, the husband's voice was little more than a hiss. "Didn't I tell you? Didn't I say something like this was going to happen?"

"We don't know why they're here." Monica sounded like she was close to tears.

"Oh yes. Yes, we do. There is no other reason for the police to be here. I said this would lead to trouble. I always knew it. That man is a menace."

Man? What man?

Charli took a tiny step closer.

"I'm not gonna pretend Chester is a good guy, but look at this house!" Monica's voice had regained some strength. "Look at what working for him got us, Tim. We both agreed to this, whatever the consequences."

Interesting. Monica was speaking in the present tense, so did that mean she wasn't aware of Crabtree's death? Or, at least, maybe she didn't want her husband to know she knew. She could have been using her words very carefully.

"I never agreed to consequences!" As Tim's footsteps moved toward the hallway, Charli stepped back, and then acted as if she was just then striding down the hall. The man's face was enraged for only a moment. As soon as he saw Charli, a warm smile took its place.

"I'm sorry about the wait. You two can come right back here. We'll talk at the dining table."

"Sounds like a plan." Charli waved Matthew forward.

While the conversation was no evidence that Monica was involved in Chester's death, it was enough information for Charli to verify that she was aware of Chester Crabtree's sketchy business practices.

The four of them sat across from each other at the long, ten-person dining room table. Charli and Matthew took the two middlemost seats while the married couple remained parallel to them.

"What exactly is this about?" Monica fidgeted with the red fabric place setting in front of her. A matching cloth napkin was gingerly folded on the other side. It was the kind of setup that Charli had only seen on special occasions, like Thanksgiving or Christmas.

"We regret to inform you that the body of Chester Crabtree was found this evening." Charli observed Monica's reaction closely.

Her lips fell open slightly, her face otherwise blank. It was a second before she spoke, and she stumbled on her words. "I-I'm sorry, did you say that Chester is dead?"

"Yes."

"Oh my god." Monica's husband reached out to wrap his arms around her. "I'm so sorry, honey."

"I don't understand. We just spoke earlier today. What happened?"

Charli wasn't prepared to give all this information away, not quite yet.

Armed with the knowledge that the Heights were already stressed about this interrogation, Charli applied further pressure. "We were hoping you might be able to tell us."

Even if Monica wasn't involved with Chester's murder, subtle allegations would only make her more eager to clear her name, potentially divulging information she would've otherwise kept close to the chest. People wanted to hide things like tax fraud, until they were accused of something as serious as murder, and then they'd sing all day about every IRS infraction they ever committed.

Monica's hand moved to her throat. "Why would I know something?"

"You were the last person to leave the parking garage this evening." Matthew placed an elbow on the table, inching forward. Charli was aware that he was on board with her tactic. Even when they didn't discuss a plan of action before going into an interrogation, they were usually on the same page. "The last person in contact with Chester's body."

"Excuse me?" Monica looked like she could hardly catch her breath. "I was never with Chester's body! I didn't even know he was dead! I don't know who you think I am, but you've got the wrong person."

"Monica, we saw your car in the parking garage and ran the plates. You are on the security feed making a phone call as you left the garage on the same level where Chester's body was found." Charli kept her tone even, not letting up. A minute from now, Monica would be eagerly revealing all she knew about Chester's financial crimes.

Monica's hands flew to her shirt collar, rubbing her neck as she tried to calm herself. "You're telling me that Chester's body was in the garage while I was there?"

Matthew's expression was cold as ice. "Chester walked down to his car just ten minutes before you left. So, yes, his body was there. Are you saying you didn't see anything at all?"

"No!" Monica shouted. Her husband was staring at her in disbelief, as if even he didn't believe she wouldn't detect such a thing. She turned to him to defend herself before facing the detectives again. "Of course I didn't! I mean, I was on the phone. I was calling my husband to tell him I was on the way back. I didn't notice anything. I was in the middle of a conversation."

Charli flipped a page in her notebook. "Monica, please take us through your day, where you were and when."

Monica bit her lip. "Let me just pause for a moment. This is such a shock. I can barely think."

Charli leaned back in her chair. "Take your time."

Monica drew in a long breath before continuing. "Okay, right, it was my day off, but Chester had some plans he wanted me to work on."

"And what exactly is your role in Crabtree's company?" Matthew asked.

"I'm his conceptual designer. He runs all the new blueprints by me, and I give my feedback. He had some plans he wanted me to look at urgently, so I promised him I'd be there after my appointment with my stylist, which wasn't over until four or so." She touched her hair, pulling on a curl. "So, I went and waited for him, but he didn't show up. That's why I was so late leaving the office. I gave up waiting."

Matthew's face remained cold as steel. "And he wanted this on your day off?"

"That's always what working for that asshole is like," Monica's husband piped up. "He expects her to be at his disposal any time of the day or night."

"Tim!" Monica glared at him. "Please! Chester's dead. Show a little respect."

Charli wasn't in the mood to listen to a lover's quarrel. "But is that true?"

She didn't much care about protecting the reputation of the dead. She only wanted as many facts on Crabtree as she could get, whether they seemed relevant to the case or not.

Monica sighed. "Yes, Chester was very particular. I won't lie and say he was easy to work for. He wasn't. But I like my job."

Charli met the woman's gaze. "Because it allows you a home as fabulous as this."

Monica's mouth cracked open. Charli had tossed out the hint that she'd heard their private conversation, and Monica caught it. The woman swallowed hard. "Chester's firm has afforded us many luxuries, yes."

"I'll be straight with you, Monica." Charli let her face go carefully blank. "We know Chester didn't operate in a moral fashion. We're not here to dig into his tax report or anything, but we do want to know if his business dealings could have led to his death."

Monica frowned. "Wait, why would the business have anything to do with his death? How exactly did he die?"

Charli weighed her options, but ultimately decided that being forthcoming would get the best reaction from Monica. "He was stabbed to death."

Tears welled in Monica's eyes. "What?"

Tim was on his feet. "What the hell? Monica, if someone killed Chester over his work, are we at risk?"

"No!" Monica pulled on her husband's sleeve. "Absolutely not. I haven't done anything that would make someone want to kill me."

"But Chester did?" Matthew leaned forward.

Monica looked like an animal caught in a corner. "No! Look, okay, I'll be honest. Yes, Chester did a lot of questionable things. Did he bribe people? All the time. Did he skirt building regulations? Yes, when he had the opportunity. But if he did something bad enough for someone to want to kill him, I don't know about it."

Just as Charli expected, the truth always surfaced when something as serious as murder was on the table. "Did you know about any plans he had for Aaron Eldridge's riverfront property?"

The woman's mouth opened and closed several times

before she licked her lips. "I only knew about them. Those were the blueprints he wanted me to look at. It's why I went to the office. He said he'd leave them on my desk, but he must have forgotten. I knocked on his office door, didn't get an answer, and I know better than to enter if his office door is shut, so I decided to wait in my office. You can check the security footage. I wasn't in the office more than a couple hours."

"What did you do while you waited?"

She frowned at Matthew's question. "I checked my emails, waiting a bit to see if Chester would come back. I was pretty pissed that I'd wasted my time." Her eyes widened. "Oh, I did see his car in the parking garage, but I didn't see him in it. That's when I went back home."

Charli made a note. "Can anyone corroborate this? Was anyone at home with you?"

She glanced at her husband. He appeared to be as eager for her answer as Charli and Matthew were. "My kids both had practice, and Tim took them because I had to go to work." Her eyes brightened. "I saw my neighbor out front. We ran into each other, complained about the landscaper we share. We both thought he'd been cutting corners. Her name is Amelia Short. She lives right across the street."

Charli jotted the name down. "All right, we'll get in contact with her. Back to those blueprints, though. Do you know anything else about Chester's plans for the riverfront property?"

"No, nothing. We didn't even get to discuss it yet."

So, Monica had a lot of information about the laundry list of crimes Chester committed, but none on the most recent property acquisition that could lead them to Bryce?

"Are you familiar with Bryce Mowery?" Even if Monica knew nothing of the riverfront property, perhaps she had seen Bryce come into the office.

"Mowery as in Montgomery Mowery?" Her nose scrunched at the name. "I know Montgomery, of course. He's our main competitor. I don't think I ever met the son."

"Did Bryce Mowery's name come up in regard to the riverfront property?" Charli watched as Monica's shoulders rose slightly and then fell in a shrug.

"Like I said, I don't know much about that property. But I can tell you that, whatever his plans were, he was extremely focused on them. He'd been holed up in his office the past week, completely focused on the acquisition. It's why I wanted to get those blueprints today. I knew how important this project was. I don't think anything was worth more to him right now than that riverfront property."

It seemed to all come back to that piece of land.

As Charli and Matthew continued to question Monica Height for another hour, one question continued to swirl in Charli's mind...

Had Chester simply been the victim of a robbery gone wrong, or was a piece of land important enough to get Chester Crabtree killed?

24

The next morning, Charli and Matthew didn't even have an opportunity to take a seat in their office when Janice Piper popped into the room.

"Ruth's been waiting for you guys to come in. She wants to see you in her office." Janice said "you guys" but only kept eye contact with Matthew.

Typical.

Charli couldn't stand this about her fellow detective. She endlessly flirted with Matthew—a fact Matthew vehemently denied—while acting like Charli was invisible.

Matthew looked longingly at his chair before heaving out a long breath. "Thanks, Janice. We'll head there right away."

"It's great to have you back, by the way." Janice flashed puppy dog eyes. "Let's grab a drink later and we can talk about your trip."

Charli turned to the wall so nobody would see her exaggerated gag. Janice never extended the invitation to Charli. Although, realistically, Charli wouldn't go even if Janice asked. The bar scene wasn't normally on her must-do list.

Ruth had her fingers on her temples at her desk when they arrived at her door.

"Is everything all right?" Matthew shut the door behind them, saving their boss from asking.

Ruth didn't answer with words, but slammed an evidence bag containing a long, silver knife onto her desk. Dried blood seemed to be glued along the edge of the blade.

"A few blocks from the parking garage, a transient noticed this in a trash can. Because it looked bloody, he called the police. The blood belongs to Chester Crabtree."

This was a huge break in the case, so why was Ruth looking so frustrated? The anger in her voice wasn't directed at them, though. Charli would know if it was. Ruth wasn't indirect about her displeasure, but something was definitely bothering her despite this valuable new piece of information.

"That's excellent." Matthew moved closer to the knife. "Do we have prints?"

"We do."

Charli had a sinking feeling that she knew the answer to the question she was about to ask, but gave it voice anyway. "But there isn't a match in the system?"

Ruth scoffed and leaned back in her chair. "Oh, there was a match all right."

Hmph. Not what she'd expected.

Charli shook off the thought and refocused on what had their sergeant so distressed. "Are you going to tell us what the problem is?"

Dark eyes locked onto Charli. "The problem, Detective Cross, is that we may have to arrest one of the richest men in Savannah. A man who plays golf with the mayor. A man I'm pretty positive is going to rain hell down on the precinct once we arrest him."

Matthew folded his arms across his chest. "Who is it?"

Charli mouthed the words at the same time Ruth said them out loud. "Montgomery Mowery."

"I knew it!" Matthew thrust his fist into the air. "Told you, Charli, I just knew. Something wasn't right about him."

Charli just stared at the knife. She agreed on that point. Something wasn't right.

"How do we have Mowery's prints?" Charli found it unlikely Montgomery had ever been printed for criminal behavior.

"He was in the military in his twenties. Navy."

This time, it was Charli pressing her fingers against her temples. "Why? Why would a smart man like Montgomery Mowery kill a man and leave fingerprints on the weapon?"

"Getting rid of his competition, of course." Matthew clapped his hands together. "First, he needed to make sure his son didn't surpass him professionally, and then he got Chester out of the way. And a man that rich is arrogant enough to think he could get away with it."

"That's a lot of conjecture." Ruth pushed to her feet. "We don't know whether Mowery killed his son, and we only know Chester's murder weapon had the man's prints on it. And I sure as hell don't want anyone walking around the precinct implying otherwise." She pointed a finger at Charli before turning it on Matthew. "The media storm is going to be bad, and Montgomery Mowery's lawyers will be all over our every move. We need to be precise in what we say. We aren't making a move until we have concrete evidence."

Matthew held up his hands in surrender, but a smirk still lingered on his lips. "Okay, fine, I won't say anything to anyone else, but come on." He let out a sarcastic chuckle. "Why would he kill Chester and not Bryce?"

Charli lifted her head. "For all we know, Chester killed Bryce, and this was Montgomery's retaliation."

Ruth nodded. "There are endless plausible scenarios, and we won't guess at them."

Charli circled back to her other question. "Would someone like Montgomery Mowery leave prints behind? He isn't a stupid man. I know he may not be a criminal mastermind, but to not wear gloves or at least wipe the weapon clean? Then just toss it in a public trash can?"

Matthew shrugged, but his excitement had dimmed at the question. "Like I said...arrogance." But Charli could tell by the look on his face that he didn't completely believe it.

"Charli's right. It's a little too convenient." Ruth gave Matthew another stern look. "Which is why we aren't rushing out to arrest Montgomery. We need to do our due diligence, and I need to talk to the prosecutor's office to see if the prints are enough to bring him in. While I do that, I need you two to go out and question him. Try to get him to come in for an official interview, but I'm sure we'll need more than this for an outright arrest."

"We can head out right now." Matthew looked eager to prove himself right.

That was the problem with gut feelings, though. Once you had one, a person sought evidence that fit their initial feeling. That kept them closed off to the world of possibilities. Matthew had it in his mind that Montgomery did this, so his viewpoint was stilted.

Charli was determined to stay open. She also wasn't choosing to believe Montgomery was innocent. It was possible he wasn't, but she had to look at all the information with a critical eye.

"In the meantime, the mayor insists on a press conference to give an update. I'm already flooded with media inquiries, even without involving Montgomery. So, if you two get stopped by a reporter, put your best face forward. Especially you, Charli."

"What's wrong with my face?" She gave a cheeky smile.

Ruth didn't smile back, and her icy stare was all Charli needed to hightail it out of the building and straight to her car. Before she could even start the engine, Matthew was reaching for the radio.

Charli groaned. "Must you?"

"Hey, I called the killer, so we have to listen to my music."

But they didn't know that, not yet. Charli didn't argue, though. The blaring country music would give her a chance to think without the chatter of conversation if it didn't give her a migraine first.

If Charli was right, and this evidence was all too convenient, it would mean someone was intentionally framing Montgomery Mowery. Although, there was still a possibility there was another killer at large. Charli reminded herself not to get tunnel vision. Like Ruth had said, there were endless possibilities. She couldn't focus on only one.

But, if these cases were linked, whoever this killer was, they liked to play games. First, by making Bryce's murder look like a suicide, then by staging an obvious murder scene with another suspect attached.

That was fine with Charli, though. Unbeknownst to the killer, playing this little game gave her a whole new set of information. And, potentially, a much smaller pool of suspects.

25

While they didn't break out the lights or sirens, not wanting to bring any extra attention to themselves, Matthew and Charli got over to the Mowery farm in record time. They caught Montgomery as he was leaving, his hand on his car door when they parked behind him.

"Excuse me, Detectives?" A twinge of an annoyance seeped through his words. "I'm going to need you to pull your car around. I have a very important appointment to get to."

"Where you headed?" Matthew stepped out of the car, ignoring Montgomery's urgency.

"I have to meet with our funeral director to approve the slide show they'll be showing at Bryce's funeral."

"I'm sorry, Mr. Mowery, but this is even more pressing than that. May we come inside?" Charli lifted a hand to shadow her eyes. The bright morning sun kept her from getting a good view of Montgomery.

Montgomery shook his head. "Doesn't really seem I have a choice, does it?"

Matthew kept his cavalier expression, but Charli didn't

share it. If Montgomery had no involvement in the deaths of either Bryce or Crabtree, it was horrific that they were about to haul him down to the station for questioning as he was making funeral arrangements. Charli found herself hoping he had a rock-solid alibi. She didn't want to make his life any harder than it had to be.

"So, what's this about?" Montgomery took them only as far as the foyer. He didn't invite them to sit down this time. Southern hospitality sometimes went out the window when grief was involved.

"We need to ask you where you were yesterday evening, between six and nine p.m." Charli shifted on her heel. She wanted to start with an alibi, so she spoke up before Matthew had a chance.

"I was at my sister's house. We had dinner, and she helped me decide on flowers and music for the funeral."

"Can anyone else corroborate that?" Matthew raised one eyebrow.

"Like, was anyone else there? No, it was just us. Why would I need to corroborate it?"

Charli inhaled deeply. That wasn't a good enough alibi to keep him out of the station. "Montgomery, last evening, we found Chester Crabtree stabbed to death in the parking garage outside of his office."

Montgomery took a step back. "Chester is dead? Do you, uh, could it be the same person who killed Bryce?"

Charli answered first. "We don't know yet, but we think that's a possibility."

It took a second for Montgomery to take in the news, but he quickly put the puzzle pieces together. "Wait, if you're asking me where I was last evening, you think I did this? Why? Why would I kill Chester Crabtree?"

"Why wouldn't you?" Matthew pressed. "He is your competition, right?"

"So? We've been competitors for more than a decade. If I was going to kill every other developer in Savannah, I'd be a serial killer."

Charli thought something similar. If Montgomery was going to oust Chester for business reasons, why now? Why wouldn't he have done something long ago?

Montgomery crossed his arms. "I have to say, Detectives, this feels very inappropriate. My son died days ago and you're out here questioning me about another murder with no evidence?"

Charli cleared her throat. "That's the issue, Mr. Mowery. We do have evidence."

A disbelieving laugh left Montgomery's lips. "What evidence?"

"The knife used to stab Chester Crabtree was found a few blocks from the crime scene with your fingerprints on the weapon."

The man appeared to be stunned. His mouth worked up and down before words escaped his throat. "That's not possible. What weapon are you talking about?"

"Do you recognize this?" Matthew held up a photo of the blood-stained knife.

The color drained from Montgomery's cheeks. "Is that a split steel knife?"

Matthew read the information at the bottom of the photo that had been collected when the item was tagged. "Yes. Do you recognize this knife?"

"Yes. I have that set."

"Are any knives missing from it?" Charli believed there was no way Montgomery could force his skin to go this pale. No, this was a real shock, though she had to admit that his surprise could have come from learning he'd been caught.

"Not that I know of, but I don't cook often."

Charli waved a hand toward the hallway she assumed led to the kitchen. "Can we go look at the set?"

Montgomery bit his lip, as if he was agonizing over allowing them farther into his home. It was obvious why. This might incriminate him.

But Charli could tell he couldn't resist looking himself. The urge was too strong. If someone had taken one of his knives to kill Crabtree, a man like Montgomery Mowery would want to know immediately.

They followed him into the kitchen, where a walnut knife block was pushed into the back corner of a countertop. Sure enough, the second space in the block was empty.

Montgomery whirled to face them. "I swear, I didn't take that out of there. Do you really think I'd do something so obvious?"

No, Charli did not. And as bad as this looked for Montgomery Mowery at the moment, it felt like a major breakthrough for Charli. Whoever framed Montgomery had access to the Mowery house.

And Charli had a feeling only a small selection of people did.

26

"God, not now." Montgomery Mowery leaned his head against his hands in frustration.

He was neither cuffed, nor was he under official arrest, but they had brought him to the precinct for official questioning. Charli hated to do this to a grieving father, but they couldn't be accused of favoritism or bowing to the rich.

A large part of her was surprised that he'd even consented to the interview. He'd had every right to refuse, and the fact that he'd come willingly won additional brownie points with Charli.

"Shit."

It wasn't immediately obvious where Mowery's frustration was coming from, but the news vans sitting in the parking lot made it clear.

"I'll take you to the rear entrance, give you some privacy."

Montgomery met Charli's eyes in the rearview mirror. "Thank you, sincerely."

"Not a problem."

From the passenger seat, Matthew side-eyed her. She knew why. He disagreed with Charli giving Montgomery any accommodations when they were hauling him in for a potential murder.

But she believed there was not a killer in the back seat, only a grieving father. Montgomery was a shrewd business-man, attentive to details. It didn't add up for him to have a knife block with a missing murder weapon sitting out in his kitchen. They would have to question him, but frankly, Charli was less interested in his alibi and far more interested in who had access to his kitchen utensils.

They pulled up discreetly, rushing Montgomery into the back door without incident. The partners escorted him into an interrogation room and left him for a moment. This wasn't unusual. It was a tactic they often used. Allowing a perp to grow anxious helped speed up the interview process.

Charli had another goal, though. She only stepped out to get on the same page as Matthew.

"I think you should inform Ruth that Montgomery is here and let me interview him alone for a bit."

"What?" Matthew let out a dry laugh. "Why wouldn't I come in with you?"

"Because I don't think you and Montgomery have the best rapport. I think he might open up to me more."

"Yeah, because you keep sucking up to him."

"Excuse me?" Charli's eyes narrowed. "I am not sucking up to him."

"Then what are you doing? Why are we dragging a rich guy in through the back so the media won't get a glimpse of him? He shouldn't get special treatment because he's loaded. Especially if he killed someone."

"I'm not giving him special treatment because he's rich!" Charli's anger echoed off the precinct walls. She attempted to make her next sentence sound calmer, lowing her voice. "I'm being kind because I actually believe he's a grieving father, not a murderer. Mowery runs a multi-million-dollar company. Do you really think he would be this careless with something as significant as murder? We saw that missing knife by waltzing into his kitchen. This screams setup to me."

Matthew's posture relaxed, and he nodded his concession of Charli's point. "Even if you're right, I don't see how me being in there can cause any harm."

"He came here willingly, and I don't want him to lawyer up. I'm sure he's got the best one in the city on speed dial. If he feels I'm on his side, maybe he'll be more cooperative about who could've had access to his kitchen."

Matthew acquiesced to Charli's strategy. "Fine, I'll catch up Ruth. But I'll be back to watch you interview him."

"Perfect. Thanks."

When Matthew was about ten feet down the hall, Charli stepped into the room where Montgomery Mowery was sitting on a metal chair. They weren't comfortable, and that was by design. The less comfortable the chairs, the more eager the suspect would be to get out of the white brick room. Besides the one-way mirror, the space felt tight and claustrophobic. Even Charli often grew uncomfortable after spending hours in here. Her hands grew sweaty when forced to interview a suspect for hours on end.

"Sorry to keep you waiting, Mr. Mowery."

His eyes were glued to his cell phone, which he slowly lowered. "My lawyer doesn't want me to speak to you."

"That is certainly within your rights." Charli didn't want to beg or coerce Montgomery. He was too smart for that. As soon as she backed him into a corner, he'd retreat. If he was going to speak to her, it had to be his idea.

"But I don't want to involve lawyers. I just want answers. I'm as surprised as you to find out a knife from my home was used to kill Chester Crabtree." The powerful man slumped, appearing almost broken from the weight of everything that was happening. "Are you going to help me get answers?"

"I want to do both. I'll be straight with you. We need to do our due diligence, and that is going to require me to ask you about your involvement with this case. But I won't stop there. We aren't looking for a scapegoat...the obvious suspect. We want justice. And that means nailing the killer."

Montgomery was quiet for a minute, silently weighing his options before he spoke again. "You're a good detective. I can see that. I saw what you did on that big case. I'll answer your questions."

"Excellent. That's very helpful, thank you." Charli withdrew her notebook and pen from her jacket. "I'll first need the name and contact information of your sister, to verify you were with her."

Charli nodded her approval when he waved his phone at her before accessing his contact information. "Emily Comstock. She's at 4731 Rareberry Lane. Number is 555-432-3521."

"And is there anyone at all who you aren't related to who could verify you were there? I know you said nobody else was present, but even a neighbor you waved to when you arrived, perhaps?"

"No, I can't think of anyone, but she'll tell you I was there. I don't understand why that isn't good enough."

She shook her head. "Family members are often willing to lie to cover for a loved one. It's not a strong alibi by itself. I'm not saying I don't believe you, but it would look better for you if you could corroborate your story in an additional way."

Montgomery nodded and released a heavy sigh. "Well, I can't remember seeing anyone else, so I don't know what to tell you."

Charli leaned back in her chair. She made a note to get a warrant to access the GPS on his car as well as his phone. She also needed to discover if the sister or any of her neighbors had cameras that might have caught Mowery entering or exiting his sister's place.

"Can you remember when that knife was last in the knife block?"

Clenching and then extending his fingers, Montgomery heaved a sigh. "Detective Cross, do I strike you as the kind of guy who cooks often…or ever? I'm barely home. I don't have any idea when those knives were last touched."

Charli had figured as much, but it never hurt to ask. The more they could narrow down the timeline, the better. Because if their only suspect couldn't give a definitive time when he last saw that knife, the case against him grew stronger.

She made another note to get the contact information of any housekeepers or anyone else who might access the home.

"You may not use those knives, but I'm sure you see them when you're in the kitchen. Think as hard as you can to the last time you saw your knife block full. Was it a week ago? A month ago? Anything you can give me would be helpful."

His gaze shifted around the room, apparently deep in thought. "Actually, yes. Sometime last month, I was making coffee and had just ground the beans when the grinder slipped from my hands, spilling grounds everywhere. I went to clean it up, and some got on the knife block, and I had to wipe down between every knife. Nothing was missing then. But besides that, I have no memory."

It was better than nothing.

"Mr. Mowery, is there anyone who would want to frame you for Chester Crabtree's death?"

"Clearly someone does, but I have no earthly idea who. I mostly keep to myself and do my work."

"Maybe that's exactly the issue, though. Maybe it has to do with your work. I hear that development companies are competitive."

He ran his hand over the edge of the cool metal table. "It is, but I don't think you're on the right track here, Detective. The development industry is competitive, yes, but it's not like we're the mafia, for god's sake. Take my son. He's dead, and yet he had no involvement in my company. Why do you automatically think Crabtree's murder was about business?"

Charli wanted to remind him that they had no official link between the deaths, but she had a bigger issue to tackle. She inhaled slowly. Charli didn't relish having to tell Montgomery that he didn't know his deceased son as well as he thought, but the truth would come out eventually. It might as well come from her.

"We have reason to think that isn't true, actually. It would appear Bryce was meeting with other influential people in the development world."

He barked out a single laugh. "I don't know who told you that, but you got your information wrong. Bryce was a lazy kid. I'd been begging him for years to take his life seriously and he never cared."

Charli looked down at her notebook. "We've heard it from multiple people, actually. His girlfriend, and his friend Roland. Several people were aware that Bryce planned to enter the business."

His eyebrows contorted. "No, but...why would he do that? Why wouldn't he tell me?"

"Perhaps he wanted to do this independently," she gently offered. "I'm sure his success would feel more satisfying without your help."

Charli had intended to lift up Montgomery, to ease him of the pain of Bryce keeping secrets from him, but this only served to push the man over the edge. Tears filled the corners of his eyes and his head dropped to the table as he cried.

"I can't do this anymore, Detective. I need to finish planning Bryce's funeral. Please, can I go? I can answer your questions later." Montgomery could only get the words out through heavy breaths.

Charli wanted nothing more than to let him go, but she desperately needed more information. She hadn't even contacted his sister to confirm the weak alibi.

"I'm sorry, but would you please stay while we confirm your story? And I still have a few more questions. But I can give you some time to yourself, if you'd like."

He nodded without looking up. Charli never knew what to do when someone was crying in front of her, so she simply got out of her seat and excused herself.

When she stepped out into the observation room, Matthew was waiting for her, staring into the one-way mirror.

"What's next, Charli?" He turned his head toward her.

"We need to get in touch with his sister to check his alibi. And after he composes himself, I'm going to find out who the hell had access to his home."

Anyone who was in that house in the past month could have taken that knife. It was a promising lead. Knowing who had access would allow them to check for possible motives.

The first glimmer of hope sparked to life within Charli. But another question began to scream louder in her mind. Was Chester Crabtree's death connected to Bryce Mowery's?

27

Matthew leaned against the brick wall as the ringing of the phone reverberated in the tight hallway space. He was making the call but put it on speakerphone so Charli could hear.

"Hello?" Emily's voice was gentle, the exact opposite of her brother's.

"Am I speaking to Emily Comstock?"

"Yes. May I ask who's calling?"

While he technically wasn't calling about Bryce's investigation, she didn't need to know that. Matthew wanted honest answers. If he told her Montgomery was currently being questioned, she might cover for him.

"This is Detective Matthew Church, and I'm investigating Bryce's death. I was hoping you could answer a few questions for me."

"Of course. Anything to help you figure out who killed my poor nephew."

"Can you run me through what you did yesterday evening?"

There was a long pause, and Matthew could practically hear the woman frown. "Why?"

"Ma'am, it would be extraordinarily helpful if you could answer the question for me."

"I'm not sure why it matters, but my brother, Montgomery, was here for dinner. He needed help with Bryce's funeral arrangements."

"Do you remember what time that was?"

"What? I don't understand. Why would you need to know that?"

"Please."

She sighed. "I didn't look at the clock or anything, but I'm guessing he was here until nine or so."

Bingo.

Matthew didn't think he'd get any further cooperation out of Emily unless he was honest. Besides, her story already seemed to line up with her brother's. No need to hide anything now.

"We need to confirm your brother's alibi regarding another homicide investigation."

The woman gasped. "Another homicide? Who else has died?"

"I'm not at liberty to discuss that at the moment. What we need to focus on right now is confirming a timeline of events regarding Montgomery's whereabouts."

"I can always send you the Ring footage from his arrival and when he left. Will that cover it?"

Matthew flashed a puzzled look at Charli, who was flipping through her little notebook. He studied the page where she'd made herself a note to check neighborhood cameras. She looked smug when she wrote the sister's name down on the page, adding a large check mark beside it.

"You have a video doorbell system?" He focused back on

the call. "Do you have any idea why your brother wouldn't mention that to us?"

"He probably doesn't know. I only got it last month, and he came in from the side yard. But you should still be able to see him entering and exiting his car. He parked right out front."

"Yes, that footage would be extremely helpful. I'll get one of our officers to drop by and copy the files, if that's all right?"

They spoke a few minutes more to make arrangements before he ended the call. Once his phone was firmly in his pocket, he finally turned to face his partner's smug expression. Though she didn't say the words, her eyes said "I told you so," even though her mouth didn't move.

"Yeah, yeah, looks like you were right again." He waved a hand toward the interview room. "You can go let him know he's free to go after you finish talking with him. We've got no grounds to detain him now."

The laws on when and for how long someone could be detained for questioning without a pending arrest were specific. Now that there was an alibi with video corroboration, keeping him longer wouldn't help their case.

"We don't need to tell him that right away, though. There are still answers we need. I don't want him running off too quickly." Charli stepped into the small observation room next to where Montgomery was sitting and looked through the window. He looked better. At least he was now sitting up in his chair, breathing slowly. "Looks like he calmed down. Want to head back in there with me?"

Matthew raised an eyebrow. "You sure I won't spook him?"

"I won't be asking about his alibi anymore, so I doubt it'll be a problem. My line of questioning will make it clear we're on his side."

They stepped through the door, and Montgomery barely made eye contact with Matthew. Charli had been right. Matthew probably shouldn't have been so icy with the guy. But in his defense, he'd truly believed that he'd been speaking to a murderer. It was hard to have empathy in that situation.

Charli sat down and leaned into the table. "Since you last saw your knife block full, who has had access to your kitchen?"

Montgomery gave it some thought. "My staff, of course. I have a housekeeper and a cook who makes meals for me five days a week. My sister and her husband came over a couple of times. Bryce would have been able to come through the house whenever he wanted, though I don't think he came up to the main house very often. Besides that, nobody."

"You don't have people over very often? No friends that stop by for dinner now and then? I know your wife passed away several years ago, but maybe even some lady friends? Even if you think someone only had access to a certain part of the house, there is always a chance they excused themselves to the bathroom and wandered about. Please consider every single house guest."

Montgomery scratched his temple. "Wait, was that…? Yes, actually, it was only three weeks ago. It feels so much longer than that now, with everything that's happened. I feel like an eternity has passed since Bryce's death. But, no, just a couple weeks ago, I did host a dinner party for the Habitat for Humanity board of directors."

"Can you tell us the exact date of this party?" Matthew folded his arms.

Montgomery opened his phone and scrolled through his calendar, giving them the date and time. "I suppose you'll want to know who was invited?"

Charli nodded. "Please."

"I'll have to send you the list, but off the top of my head, most of the board members are local development and real estate professionals." He scratched his chin. "You know the saying about keeping your friends close and enemies closer? That's why I try to have little get togethers like this."

That was interesting. "Do you consider your fellow development and real estate professionals to be your enemies?"

Montgomery shrugged. "Not mortal enemies, if that's what you're saying, but competitors for sure. A lot of money is on the line for some of these pieces of land. They don't say money is the root of all evil for nothing."

The man sure did like his cliches.

Charli and Matthew stayed silent, waiting him out. Montgomery threw up his hands. "There have been fights, arguments, that sort of thing. And being that I've got the biggest company in the city, I try to lead by example."

"Can you toss out a few of the names who attended the party?" Charli was poised to write each name down.

Montgomery rattled off about ten names, but only three that Matthew immediately recognized: Chester Crabtree, Jack Derringer, and Aaron Eldridge.

"How well do you know Derringer and Eldridge?" Charli looked up at him after jotting everyone down.

"I know Jack Derringer very well. He's on the city committee that approves all new development projects. I try to stay on that man's good side. He gets a lot done. I don't know Aaron Eldridge at all, so I didn't even invite him."

"You didn't? Then why was he there?" Matthew asked.

"He was a guest of Chester Crabtree. I assumed that was because Chester had just got his bid accepted on the riverfront property. I didn't ask many questions. I never do…" he pursed his lips together, "*did* with Chester. That man's motives are always so convoluted, it's best to keep your distance."

This riverfront property continued to pop up. Charli

wanted to get to the bottom of who had taken the knife, but even when they discovered that, they'd need to find a motive. And Matthew strongly suspected that motive was wrapped in this sale of land. He needed to understand more about how these sales operated.

"Can you explain to me what exactly happens when someone wants to sell a large piece of property like Eldridge did?"

Montgomery finally made eye contact with Matthew. "Well, they'll have their commercial real estate agent announce the potential sale, and any development company that is interested will set up a proposal and bid for the property. Their proposal has to be approved by a committee prior to the closing of the sale, so committee approval is vital. Once proposals are approved, the seller is free to choose the most attractive bid."

"And in the case of Eldridge's property, you weren't aware of any bid that Bryce made?" Matthew leaned back in his chair.

"No. Look, I know you guys have told me Bryce was interested in the development business, but I think the idea that he would create a proposal is a bit of a stretch. That's a hell of a lot of work."

But according to Derringer, Bryce had drawn up a proposal, and a damn good one. Though it was clear Montgomery Mowery knew nothing about it.

Matthew knew two people who would, though. Jack Derringer and Aaron Eldridge had some questions to answer.

M edia vans were already in the parking lot when I arrived. I didn't want to hang too close and risk being seen, so I found a space toward the back of the lot. There were several civilian vehicles in the spaces in addition to a number of patrol cars. This was likely the place anyone who worked at the precinct parked.

I leaned back in my seat, keeping my head down without seeming too obvious about it. I was pleased to see that the local news was already out. They'd get word out about who was in custody and spin the story to the public. Montgomery Asshole Mowery would soon go from beloved public figure to loathed by the entire city in twenty-four hours.

Though I had to wonder, how exactly would the story play out? Montgomery would be marked as Chester's murderer. That much I knew. But what about Bryce? I had hoped from the beginning that Bryce's death would be ruled a suicide, but the cops knew that wasn't true. As unlikely as it might be, I could only hope they'd pin that murder on Montgomery as well. It wasn't like those two weren't constantly fighting.

More likely, they might assume Chester was responsible for Bryce's demise. A father avenging his son would make good media fodder. I needed to plant that story in some reporter's ear if the talking heads didn't jump to that conclusion soon.

I'd have to plug into the five o'clock news to find out. Either scenario suited me just fine. It took Bryce, Chester, and Montgomery out of the game. That was all that mattered. Now that they had all been eliminated, I could end this parade of death.

A slow sigh escaped me. I wasn't ready for it to end. At the onset, I'd planned to accumulate an unfathomable amount of wealth. It would lead to power and a level of success I'd never had before. Before killing Bryce, the only way I viewed power was through financial domination.

That had all changed.

This experience had given me a drastically different mindset. Money wasn't the only way to obtain power. Perhaps it wasn't even the best way. Watching someone's soul leave their body was so much more impactful than staring at my bank account.

It made me a god. A supreme entity who controlled both life and death.

I wanted more. I just needed someone, anyone, to give me another excuse to feel that way again.

And I knew exactly who that person needed to be…her. She'd kept some secrets from me. But because I planned to keep her around initially, I didn't have an easy way to oust her right now. So that would have to wait, potentially for a long time. At least until I was out of Savannah, safe from the grips of the local police. The dust would have to settle on Bryce and Chester's cases before I could give her what she deserved.

What *I* deserved.

I was staring out at the intersection, watching rows of cars flow by, when a vehicle finally turned into the lot. I leaned forward to get another view, but the car zoomed past so quickly I couldn't make out who was inside. There were two people in front and one in back, but that was as much detail as I got.

I pulled out my phone and scrolled through my contacts. He answered on the second ring. "Hello, Larry speaking."

"Larry, it's me. I saw your news van at the precinct right now. I just drove by and was wondering what was going on?"

Larry was the father of one of the kids I went to high school with. We weren't close, but since I became a multi-millionaire, people I knew even casually were suddenly willing to do me favors.

"I don't have an official source yet, but word on the street is Montgomery Mowery is being hauled in. Not sure for what, though."

That was all I needed to know. "Interesting. Thanks, Larry." I hung up before he even had time to say another word. I had another call to make.

"It's done. They've got Montgomery Mowery in custody. Everything ready on your end? We need to get the hell out of here, now."

29

T he repetitive ringing was tedious in Charli's ear. So many calls, but she wasn't any closer to an answer. This was by far the worst part of the job.

She hated speaking to people on the phone. She'd much rather surprise a potential suspect or even a witness and watch their initial reaction to her presence as well as inspect their body language while they answered questions. But Aaron Eldridge was a hard man to find.

"Hello, Aaron speaking."

Finally.

"Hello, Mr. Eldridge, this is Detective Charli Cross with the Savannah Police Department. I would like to meet with you to ask you a few questions."

"I-I…" Eldridge stuttered on the other end of the line. "I'm sorry. Did you say you were with the police department? Why do you want to meet with *me?*"

"We believe you may have relevant information to a case we're working on. I've been told you recently sold a strip of coveted riverfront property."

"I did, but I don't understand how that could be of any concern to the police."

"Sir, the sale of the property might not have anything to do with our case, but we're attempting to be thorough. Where would you like to meet? I'm happy to come to you, or you're welcome to meet with me here at the precinct."

Charli held her breath while the man made the decision.

"Well, I suppose I could give you a few minutes of my time. I'll be available at around five p.m. Can you meet me at the Indigo Air Tearoom? I have a meeting there soon afterward."

Admittedly, Charli was sick of these elitist downtown businesses, but she agreed. It was going to be enough of a pain trying to get these rich business owners to make time to meet with them. They'd have to take any opportunity they could.

Five o'clock was several hours away, so Charli and Matthew took the time to call the other guests on their list to schedule meeting times. Some of them had to conduct interviews by phone because they were on vacation. They'd managed to get two of those phone interviews done by four-thirty. Neither turned up any relevant information.

Charli slammed her phone down on the receiver. The sound was satisfying, and she wished there was a slamming option on her cell phone too.

Matthew arched an eyebrow and raised his arms over his head for a long stretch. "Sick of phone calls? Me too. Sometimes, I'm not sure if I'm a detective or a telemarketer."

"No, it's not that. It's just...it's going to take so long to verify alibis. And we can only hope that someone saw something suspicious because we've got no additional prints on the knife."

"Chin up there, Detective. They're still testing the knife block itself. We could find prints on that."

But Charli thought this unlikely. Whoever killed Crabtree had covered their tracks well. They wouldn't make such a fatal mistake.

"No more phone interviews." Charli pushed the offending device to the edge of her desk. "If someone says they're out of town, schedule something for when they come back. We need to be drilling these people in person if we have any hope of getting someone to crack."

"You got it." Matthew tapped his desk. "Hey, should we head out to that tearoom now? I could use an iced sweet tea."

Charli glanced back at Matthew. His forehead was dripping with perspiration. His desk was right next to the window, so his seat was in direct sunlight. And the AC vent was to the right of Charli's desk, so most of the air blew on her. She felt for him. It was annoying enough to schedule these meetings even when the sun wasn't beating down on you.

Still, she had to laugh. "I don't think sweet tea is the kind of thing they serve."

His eyes widened then narrowed. "They better have iced tea of some kind."

"Grab a Coke out of the vending machine on our way out, just in case they don't."

Matthew did just that, and by the time they reached the car, Charli was regretting not taking her own advice. That damn office AC could be so deceptive. How'd it blow so cold when the humid air outside was sweltering? She wiped her forehead before getting into her car.

"You think Eldridge will have anything valuable for us?" Matthew raised his window. The AC needed time to cool down the interior.

"He'll at least give us more insight into what role Bryce may have had with this riverfront property. So far, it seems only Blair and Jack Derringer know about Bryce's bid. I'm sure he'll have more details on that front."

Though, with the information they had now, it didn't seem likely Eldridge was their murderer. If Bryce bid on the property and Chester Crabtree got it, what possible reason would Eldridge have to murder either of them? His goal was to make money off them, right?

The tearoom was dimly lit, the walls covered in a black floral wallpaper. A hostess stand was set up in front, where a petite woman with a black bob smiled at Matthew and Charli.

"Do you have a reservation?" She opened a maroon book and started running her finger down the page.

"No, we don't, actually." Charli was about to explain they were meeting someone when the hostess chimed in.

"Oh, I'm so sorry, but you have to have a reservation. Even during the week, we often fill up and—"

"They're with me, Cherry."

Charli followed the voice and found a curly haired blond man smiling at them. His baby face made him look like he was in his mid-twenties while his khaki pants and blue blazer aged him a bit.

"Aaron Eldridge?" Matthew looked him up and down.

"That's me. Please, Detectives, come take a seat."

They followed him to a table where he already had a black teapot and three cups set out. Charli would definitely not be partaking in any hot tea and had no idea how Eldridge could stand something so warm in this weather.

"So, Detectives, what can I help you with?" Aaron flashed a shiny smile. His teeth were impeccably white even in the badly lit room.

"We want to ask you about the riverfront property you put up for sale."

"That I sold to Chester Crabtree? Of course, I just heard

an hour ago of his passing. So tragic. We just closed the sale last weekend. I was really looking forward to seeing that neighborhood come to life under his plan."

"What was his plan, exactly?" Charli asked.

"He wanted to devise a high-end shopping center of sorts. The location was perfect for it."

A shopping center, huh? That sounded awfully close to Bryce's plan for an open-air mall.

Charli was about to ask about Bryce's plan when Matthew gave the man a hard look. "Were you aware of Chester Crabtree's questionable business practices?"

Aaron Eldridge stared at him, squinting in confusion. "Like what, exactly?"

"Bribes, cutting corners on construction work, black-mailing committee members."

Eldridge's expression fell. "Chester Crabtree did all that? No, sorry, I wasn't aware. If I'm being honest, I'm new to the world of development. I only recently inherited this land and have little experience with selling property. Chester simply offered the largest amount of money, by far, and I took it. Though I have to say, Chester always seemed nice to me. After I sold him the land, he started taking me under his wing. He even invited me to join the Habitat for Humanity board of directors. I met a number of developers on the board and was even invited to Montgomery Mowery's exclusive dinner party."

Charli glanced at Matthew before speaking up. "We wanted to ask you about that too. Was that your first time at the Mowery household?"

"In the main house, yes. But I was friends with Bryce, and he'd invited me back to his home a few times. Bryce was at the party briefly, but he didn't stay too long. I think those parties bored him. Not that I could blame him. It kind of bored me too."

"Why did you go?" Matthew asked.

Aaron looked at Matthew as if he couldn't believe he'd asked such a question. "I wanted to make connections, of course. Now that I'd come into so much money from Crabtree's deal, I was considering starting my own business. I saw it as a networking opportunity."

"Did you?" Charli watched the man closer. "Make connections?"

And happen to snatch a knife from the kitchen?

Aaron shrugged. "Nobody talked about business much. Everyone just kind of mingled and ate hors d'oeuvres between cocktails."

"Was the party contained to one area or did people mingle throughout the house?" Charli hoped it wasn't the latter. Their investigation would be more difficult if the guests had free access to the kitchen.

"No, we were all in the parlor. Caterers brought in food and drink."

"And did anyone leave the parlor?" It was a question Charli planned to ask every guest to discover if anyone had sneaked off.

"Not that I can remember, but I wasn't taking notice. I'd gotten a little tipsy."

Matthew opened his notepad. "Can we get a list of everyone who made a bid for your land?"

Eldridge seemed taken aback. "Uh, is that necessary? That information is private, not to be disclosed publicly."

His reaction was curious, and Charli leaned in. "Why can't it be disclosed publicly?"

"Because the bids are sealed for a reason. From what I understand, if someone pitches a project and doesn't get it, they may still want to use those ideas to develop another piece of land. They wouldn't want to give their competitors access to their plans."

"We don't need to see the actual plans. You can just give us the names if that puts your mind at ease." Charli used a softer tone than usual. Best to make a polite request so she could get her information without a warrant.

"Okay, I guess I can send you an email. But I don't understand why you need the info."

Matthew's tone harshened, and Charli could tell it was in response to Eldridge's blasé attitude. "Do you think there's anyone who would want to kill either Bryce Mowery or Chester Crabtree over this strip of land?"

Aaron, who had been in the middle of sipping his tea, nearly spit it out. "Of course not! Why would they?"

Matthew shrugged. "We keep hearing that development competition is brutal. Maybe someone else really wanted a shot at your property."

"But that doesn't even make sense. How would Bryce's death have anything to do with my property?"

Charli jerked her head up. "Wait, are you saying Bryce never put a bid on the riverfront land?"

"Bryce? Are you kidding?" Aaron chuckled. "Why would you even think that? Look, I liked Bryce. We hung out sometimes, but he wasn't interested in working. I don't think he's ever drawn up a land proposal in his life."

If that was true, that changed the entire course of their investigation. But it made little sense. According to Blair, Jack Derringer told her Bryce had a proposal for the property. Not only that, but Bryce had set up a meeting about it between Crabtree, Eldridge, and himself. Someone was lying.

They needed to get in touch with Jack Derringer.

"What about Chester, though?" Charli asked. "In the event of his death, would someone else get a chance at the land?"

"No, definitely not. We already closed before he died. It's sold to Crabtree Industries. His company is responsible for the property." Aaron shook his head. "I don't see how there could be a financial gain to killing Chester, at least not in regard to my property. Maybe there is another coveted piece of land that could be responsible for his death."

Charli had high hopes for this interview but was only left with a longer list of questions. Had Blair's information been reliable at all? Maybe she had made it up, or Jack Derringer had. And if that was the case, they were basically back to square one.

She made a note to follow up with the tech department to see if they'd found anything on Chester's computer that could be helpful.

Right now, the only tie that Bryce had with Chester was this strip of property. If Bryce was never involved, the two murders could be entirely unrelated. Or the motive could be personal in nature, as opposed to financial. It would be back to the drawing board if Blair lied.

And if that young woman had lied? Charli would toss every charge of obstruction she could think of at her purple head.

On the other hand, if Blair and Derringer had been telling the truth, then Aaron Eldridge may know a lot more about both of these murders than he was letting on. Someone wasn't being honest, and if it was Eldridge, what was his motive for lying?

"So, where exactly were you on the night of Bryce's murder?" Charli's tone was normal, but her eyes drilled into Eldridge.

The sustained eye contact made him uncomfortable, and he looked down at his tea. "I was in New York City, actually."

Matthew cocked his head. "What's in New York?"

"A friend. I'm new to all these business dealings, but I have a friend from college who went into finance law. To celebrate the sale, I thought a trip to New York would be fun, and along the way, I visited with him to get some advice on good investments for my new windfall. I can get you his contact info to verify I was there."

"Yeah, we'll need that." Matthew's cold response should have cooled the pot of tea between them. "What about last night between six and nine p.m.?"

Aaron's eyes widened, and his face reddened. "I was with a, um, friend."

"We'll need to know your friend's name along with that list of bidders and their proposals." Charli gave him a stern look. "Don't forget."

"No, I won't. As soon as I'm done with my meeting here in a little bit, I'll send the list of names right over." Aaron checked his watch. "You'll have to excuse me, Detectives, but I do believe that is my guest at the door. If you have any other questions, I'll be happy to answer them later."

Matthew turned to examine the newcomer. "Who is your guest, exactly?"

"Thomas Payne, an old friend from my school days. He's been wanting to get dinner for a while. I don't want to keep him waiting."

"Sure." Charli stood and pushed her business card across the table. "If you think of anything that might be pertinent to our case, big or small, please contact us. We'll be in touch."

She meant that. Charli expected she'd be giving Aaron Eldridge a call very soon.

Right after they spoke to Jack Derringer.

30

The second they left the tearoom, Charli insisted on finding Derringer straight away. In fact, she already had the car turned on and the thing in drive before Matthew settled his ass into his seat.

"But I already had an interview scheduled with one of the guests for six tonight." Matthew put on his seat belt and rolled down his window. Though they'd only been inside the tearoom for about fifteen minutes, the car was already sweltering again. The heat of the seat nearly seared his skin through his pant leg.

"That will have to wait." Charli thrust the transmission back into park and turned up the air conditioner, blowing even more hot air in Matthew's face. "We know that either Eldridge or Derringer is lying to us. If it's Derringer, it throws the whole damn investigation for a loop. But if it's Eldridge, then he's hiding something, and we need to come at him harder."

Matthew didn't need to hear more. "If Eldridge is involved, then our little chat might have spooked him."

"Exactly." Charli tapped the steering wheel with her

thumbs. "He's got millions of dollars. We don't need him fleeing the country."

Something didn't add up, though. "Look, I'm not saying the kid isn't sketchy. I didn't like his demeanor or his attitude. But what we're missing here is a motive. Why would Eldridge want to kill either Mowery or Crabtree?"

"We can always discover the motive later, after we figure out if he's lying to us."

Matthew attempted to turn his favorite radio station on again, but Charli slapped his hand away.

"Nuh uh, you said you got to choose the music because you were right about Montgomery. Well, you weren't, so winner gets to pick."

Matthew tightened his lips to hold back the growing smile. "You really wanna rub that one in, huh?"

"Sure do."

Her short hair waved in the wind as she rolled the car forward with her window down. He couldn't help but admire her. Despite him having ten years of service on her, in many ways, she was a more effective detective than he was.

It didn't make Matthew jealous, but proud. She was his partner, and her ingenuity often helped them solve a case. Of course he liked to think the way they pushed each other fueled that ingenuity. Either way, no one could deny they were one hell of a team.

Matthew was grateful this case didn't dredge up old wounds for Charli. It had been hard to watch her struggle on the last case as so many young women turned up dead. A relentless parade of painful memories of her friend who'd been murdered haunted her each time a new young female victim was found. Charli didn't deserve to relive that pain.

"You seem better." Matthew shifted in his seat uncomfortably, realizing that may not be something Charli wanted to hear. "I mean, I know our last investigation got to you." That sentence didn't make the original statement sound any better.

Charli side-eyed him. "Me, huh? Weren't you the one who fled to the other side of the country afterward?"

Her tone was teasing, so she wasn't mad. "Yeah, well, I guess that investigation was hard on me too. I kept thinking of Chelsea, you know? She's young, and I'm unable to protect her from so far away. I'd murder anyone who laid a hand on her."

Charli let out a sad sigh. "I know. It was hard on all of us. Probably why we've all discussed it so little. Nothing to do but move on, right? Gotta be onto the next one."

And onto the next one they were.

They arrived at a light blue home with a detached garage. Matthew knew this part of town. Most of the houses were built in the 1930s, before it was normal to attach a garage to every middle-class family home. Of all the houses they'd seen so far, Derringer's was by far the most modest.

Charli was thinking the same thing. "I guess being a committee member doesn't pay as well as owning a development company."

"No kidding. I could probably afford this place on my salary. Well, if alimony and child support didn't drain it."

Charli glanced around. "No car to be seen."

"He could have parked in the garage."

They knocked on the door several times, to no avail. Charli put her ear to the door, attempting to hear any noises inside. Seeing cops at the door scared off many people, so he could be refusing to answer while hiding in some corner.

"Hear anything?"

Charli shook her head. "Nothing. Maybe he's at work. We could call down to his office and—"

Matthew's phone interrupted Charli mid-sentence.

"It's Janice." Matthew turned the speakerphone on after picking up. "Hello?"

"Uh, hey, how far from the precinct are you?"

"About twenty minutes, why?"

"You're going to want to come down here. Our anonymous tip email account just received something about your case. Subject header is 'Eldridge's Land.'"

31

Charli hovered over Matthew's shoulder. "Can't this thing load any faster?"

"We're a government agency, Charli. No room in the budget for high-speed internet." The attached images of the plans made the connection all the more sluggish.

Charli's heart had been pounding since Janice's call. It was the familiar surge she experienced before discovering a potential lead. She'd wanted nothing more than to speed back to the precinct, sirens blazing, but she had a moral objection to breaking traffic laws. Other cops might believe they were above the law, but Charli didn't.

So, she drove the agonizing twenty minutes back to the precinct, wondering what the email said. It would be more convenient if they could check the tip email from their own devices, but it was connected to the department's server and couldn't be accessed elsewhere to maintain cyber security. Which reminded Charli...

"Janice remembered to forward this to Cyber, right? Have they got an IP address?"

Matthew waggled his eyebrows. "Why don't you run out and ask her yourself?"

He wanted Janice and Charli to get along, be friends, but that wasn't going to happen. If Janice wanted to fawn over her partner, there was no reason Matthew shouldn't be the one to communicate with her. After all, it was Matthew's phone Janice called, not Charli's. It was Matthew she told to get back to the precinct. She didn't even mention Charli, though she knew they were doing interviews together.

Finally back in their office, Matthew leaned into the screen, and Charli followed suit. "Wait, I think it's almost loaded."

When the image popped up, neither knew what they were looking at. It was some kind of blueprint, but of what?

"Wait, zoom into the top right corner. I think something is scribbled there." Charli pointed to the writing too small to read. But when Matthew enlarged the image, the words became clear.

"This was Bryce's proposal for an open-air mall on Eldridge's new strip of land. I thought the police should be aware of its existence."

There was no signature under the cursive message, but the information could not have come at a better time.

"So, if this is true, Aaron Eldridge *was* lying to us."

Charli met her partner's gaze. "But why?"

Charli racked her brain. She didn't see any obvious reason to hide that Bryce Mowery had placed a bid on the land. Sure, he had been hiding his interest in working from his father, but why go so far to cover up his dealings?

"Maybe Eldridge didn't want to tell us so we wouldn't think he was involved in his death?" Matthew offered.

"But that makes no sense. Just because someone puts a bid out for your land doesn't mean you want to kill them. If he didn't want to sell the land to Bryce, just don't sell the land to Bryce. There is no sense in killing him."

"People have killed for less."

That was certainly true, and no response came readily to Charli's tongue.

Luckily, a knock on the door halted the conversation. It was Janice.

"Sorry to interrupt." She smiled at Matthew. "Just wanted to let you know, the cyber guys found an IP address, but it only led to a VPN. All the metadata was wiped from the photo as well. Whoever sent this did not want to be found."

And that only complicated matters further. Why was someone being so secretive about getting them this information? Did they think someone would retaliate?

"You think this could be Jack Derringer?" Matthew crossed his arms and turned his chair to face Charli after Janice left.

"Why do you say that?"

"He's got this information, and he doesn't seem too keen on talking to us."

Charli shrugged. "Maybe he wasn't home."

"It's not just that. It's that he didn't call the department to begin with. Why would Derringer spill his secrets to Blair Daughtry instead of the police? What's he afraid of?"

Being fearful of interacting with the police was one explanation, but Charli wondered how much farther his reticence went. "But Blair said Derringer was afraid Chester would retaliate against him. Chester is dead. Who is he afraid of now?"

"I don't know." Matthew pushed to his feet with a long groan. "But there's one way to find out."

32

Three suitcases were open on my bed. I had meticulously packed them a week ago but felt compelled to go through them once more.

A week ago, I was only packing for a vacation. I hoped I still was. But I worried more and more that I hadn't covered my tracks. If I hadn't, this trip would become permanent, so I sorted through my belongings to make sure I wasn't leaving behind anything that couldn't be replaced.

Though, with the kind of money I had now, most anything was replaceable. My original plan had been to stay in Savannah, to work my way up to being the richest man in this city, but plans could always be adjusted.

Hell, maybe that dream was too small for me, anyhow. The person who decided it would be sufficient to succeed in Savannah, he was only a boy. He hadn't made the kind of decisions yet that turned him into a man. Ending people's lives gave me perspective.

A big part of me didn't think I'd be happy with making money anymore. Sure, that could play a part in my goal to feel all-powerful, but it wasn't the only thing I needed. If I stayed in the U.S., I would have very few opportunities to… enjoy my new hobby. The police here were fastidious, and if more bodies were discovered, the Feds would get involved. If that happened, getting caught was a matter of when, not if.

Where I was going in Mexico, though, it would be different. Murders went unsolved all the time down there. The cartel ran entire cities on fear alone. They made people like Montgomery Mowery look like pussies.

Perhaps I wasn't made for this city, but for something bigger. I wasn't a Mowery. I was an Escobar. A man of power. I was in the process of amassing wealth that guys like Crabtree could only dream of. Nobody in the upper crust of Savannah had the balls to make that kind of cash.

Except for me.

I was better than all of them, and I'd prove it. Hell, the threat of getting caught could be the best thing that ever happened to me, forcing me to leave this city. If it kept me from being able to return to the States, forcing me into a new life, maybe that was for the best.

I didn't know if she was ready for that, though. I knew her. To her, this was still a leisurely trip to Cancun. She didn't want to stay out of the U.S. permanently.

But it wasn't up to her. She was just another pawn in my chess game, someone I could choose to keep or sacrifice to win. Her role was useful enough for a while that I had thought I'd keep her.

Her betrayal changed that, though. You couldn't play both sides, not with me. It was easy to see her for who she truly was, just another gold-digging whore who was willing to latch onto whatever man came out victorious.

It was disgusting how women could do that. They talked about feminism and wanting equality, but most of them were out to find a man they could latch onto for financial security. They didn't get down and do the work themselves. They didn't take on the real risk. Because if the man they chose failed, they could run off and find another.

I'd hoped she'd be different, and she'd be willing to take part. If I was going to keep a woman around, she needed to be willing to get her hands dirty. But in retrospect, I was still the one making and executing the plan. She did so little and still managed to deceive me while doing it.

Even if I never got caught and decided it was safe to return to Savannah, she wouldn't be returning with me. That much I knew. So, I'd add at least one more body to my count by the end of this, though I still craved so much more.

What would it feel like if, by the end of my lifetime, I'd played god to thousands? My name would strike fear into the hearts of people. More than Dahmer or Bundy could ever dream.

As I sifted through piles folded of shirts, one of my bags vibrated. I slid it to the left to reveal my burner phone underneath.

It was her.

"Hello?"

"Any chance you can move our flights up?" Her tone was urgent, desperate. I took a deep breath and wondered if this was how she'd sound in her last moments. Only time would tell.

"Why? We're leaving at ten tonight. Is that not good enough for you?"

"Things have changed. I think we should leave sooner."

I sat on the edge of my bed. "Why don't you just slow down and tell me what you're worried about."

She blew out a frustrated breath. "Have you not been checking the key logger?"

"Not today." *What had I missed?* "I had several meetings to attend to, so I've been busy."

"Well, I haven't, and he's sent an email to the police. They have Bryce's proposal."

Shit. That threw a wrench into my plans

Though it also opened up a new possibility, and the chance to play god one more time before wrapping this all up.

"There's no need to rush. We can still leave as scheduled."

"What?" She gasped. "Are you listening to me? The cops could be on their way already!"

"And that is fine. We'll get there first. You ready to make a quick pit stop before we leave town?"

There was silence on the other end. She tried to act hard, like she was down for anything, but I knew that wasn't true. I'd know if she was a cold-blooded killer. She didn't have the heart for this.

Still, she agreed, because gold-digging whores always did.

She giggled. "For the amount of cash we'll be rolling in, you can make as many stops as you want."

Atta girl.

33

B eads of sweat dripped down her forehead as Charli glared at Derringer's secretary as she told them that she wasn't at liberty to divulge her boss's personal business.

They'd tried his offices first, knowing that businessmen tended to keep long hours. So did their assistants.

Charli had given her a hard look, while beside her, Matthew did the same. "This is important."

The secretary lifted her chin. "Do you have a warrant or a subpoena or anything that suggests you have a legal reason to connect with him?"

Charli wanted to punch her. Instead, she flipped a card on her desk. "Let me know if you hear from him. We need to get in touch with him ASAP." Frustration seeped out of her in the form of a long huff as they walked back outside.

Matthew shook his head. "Guess they don't call them the gatekeepers for nothing."

Charli pulled her shoulders back, hoping to stretch out the knot tightening her muscles. "She said she hadn't seen him all day. Do you think he skipped town?"

"Could explain his car being gone."

Damn it.

They were closer than ever to getting some answers, and the one person who could provide them had disappeared. Worse…someone might have made them disappear.

She sighed and wiped her sweaty forehead with her sleeve. "It could also mean that we have another dead body to find."

"We could go back to Derringer's house again," Matthew suggested.

"And do what? We don't have cause to enter uninvited. We have no warrant, he's not under arrest, and nobody has called to express concern for a wellness check."

Matthew gave her a smug grin. "Who's to say someone didn't call about a wellness check?"

"No!" Charli was defiant. "We can't do that. These laws exist for a reason. I'm not going to break them because we want to solve this case quickly."

But boy, she wanted to. A chilled silence hung in the air. They could continue to go down their list of other house guests from Mowery's dinner, but that felt pointless now that they knew Eldridge was lying. He'd been dishonest for a reason. Charli needed to discover that reason.

Charli ran her fingers through her short hair, a move she only ever made in frustration. It was an action Matthew knew well. Charli was never loud in her irritations…it wasn't her way. He was the hothead of their team while she kept her cool in nearly every situation.

But the sun was beating down, causing sweat to form in the underarms of her shirt. The September temperature was wearing her down, and she was already exhausted from their previous investigation. Statistics showed that crime rates actually increased when the weather got hot, so it wasn't just Charli being driven mad by the heat.

"Why don't we go grab some milkshakes, try to figure out

a way we can reach Derringer, and then plan our next move?" It was like their roles had reversed. Matthew was putting in the effort to calm her down while Charli struggled to manage her agitation.

"Doesn't this frustrate you?" Charli slammed her door shut, ready to drive to the local Dairy Queen.

"Of course it does, but we're heading toward a milk-shake." His lips quirked. "Milkshakes are my zen."

Charli wished her zen could be found as easily.

"I need a vacation."

Matthew shot her a look. "You need to talk to your dad."

That took the wind out of her. Yeah, she did. But after her disaster of a dinner with him Sunday night, she had no desire to talk to him at the moment.

"We both need to do a lot of things. Let's get those milkshakes."

Matthew shrugged. He and she both knew that she wouldn't take a vacation any time soon. In fact, she hadn't taken one since she started at the precinct. There wasn't any place she particularly wanted to go, and she didn't have a friend or boyfriend to go with. What was she going to do? Run away to some tropical paradise alone?

Actually, that didn't sound half bad. It would be a pleasant change of pace to read her crime books on a beach instead of in her living room. Still, Charli wouldn't do it. Because if she slowed down in her work, she'd be pulled into her worst thoughts. It wouldn't be much of a vacation if nightmares of her childhood friend plagued her the entire time.

Charli ordered a cookies and cream shake while Matthew got strawberry. They sat in the parking lot, AC blasting as hard as it could, and sucked thick drinks through straws.

Matthew smacked his lips. "Okay, so we've left messages on his home and cell. We visited his office, and they haven't seen him all day. He didn't answer the door. What options do we have?"

Charli waited for an answer to come to her as the cool, sweet liquid slid down her throat. It was amazing how a cold drink could cool down the entire body. Her irritation slowly disappeared with each sip.

"What about Blair Daughtry? It didn't seem like she was close to Derringer, but maybe she knows something about where he's gone."

"Or wasn't telling us the whole story." Charli kicked herself internally for her obliviousness. "I should have already thought of that."

"You can't be the genius all the time. Sometimes I gotta do some work too, ya know."

Charli pressed the cold cup to her forehead. "Agree to disagree. I'm always the genius. Except when the heat has cooked my brain."

"Whatever you gotta tell yourself, Charli."

A van from a local news station pulled into the parking lot, and Charli instinctively sank into her seat.

Matthew frowned and followed her line of sight. "Relax. They're probably just wanting a milkshake too."

Charli hoped so. She hated the spotlight.

She put the car into drive. "Let's not tempt fate."

But before she pulled out, she dialed Blair's number. Her phone automatically connected to the car speakers. Blair answered almost immediately.

"Hello?"

Charli looked both ways before rolling the car forward. "Blair, it's Detective Cross. Glad I could catch you. I was wondering if you could put me in touch with Jack Derringer."

Silence.

"Blair? You still there?" Charli's heart rate accelerated

when she didn't get a response. Had something happened on the other end of the line?

"I'm here." She offered no further explanation.

"Okay, so, can you help me get in touch with Derringer? Do you know where he is?"

"I do."

Why the hell was the girl being so cryptic? "Okay, so where is he?"

"I don't think I can tell you. I don't think he wants you to know."

"Why not?"

More silence.

"Blair, this is vitally important."

"He doesn't want to talk to the police. He made that very clear to me. Jack thinks he's in danger and if he's seen speaking to you, it could get bad for him."

"He very well may be in danger. Which is why it's important that we get ahold of him. When did you last talk to him, and who does he think is after him?"

Blair sighed. "He called a little while ago, freaking out about everything he told me. He made me promise not to say anything to anyone."

Charli closed her eyes. "Did you tell him that you'd already spoken to us?"

"No." The word was small.

"Does he suspect who might be after him?"

"He wouldn't tell me. At first, he said that he thought it was one of Crabtree's goons that went after Bryce. Now that Chester is dead too, he's so scared he won't even leave his house."

"Wait, so he *is* at his house?"

"Shit." Blair realized her mistake. "Okay, yeah, fine. Jack called me about an hour ago and told me he was packing to leave. He's getting out of town. I think he's real worried about his safety now."

Derringer wasn't going anywhere until Matthew and Charli could speak to him first. "Thanks."

She was about to end the call when Blair cried out, "Please don't go over there, sirens blazing. He doesn't want to draw unwanted attention."

"I promise, we'll be discreet."

Charli hung up and looked over at Matthew as she pulled out of their parking space.

He was staring back at her. "You sure you don't want to run over there with sirens? We should be quick. Blair is definitely going to call him back and he might get out of dodge fast."

Charli considered this. "But what if we make our presence obvious? He'll be even more reluctant to answer the door. If he's that worried about being seen speaking to us, he'll refuse to talk. And we still don't have any legal reason to force entry."

The car speakers began to ring, and Charli looked down at her phone to see if Blair was calling back. But she wasn't. It was Matthew getting a call this time. He pushed his phone on the car's touchscreen to answer.

"Detective Church."

Janice's breathing was heavy. "Dispatch just got a call from Jack Derringer. He says someone is trying to break into his house. We've already sent two cars."

Matthew glanced at Charli. "Thanks, Janice, we'll be right there."

Charli pressed her foot on the gas. "I guess we've got a reason to enter now."

34

Despite Charli's visible anxiety on the way to Derringer's home, Matthew was filled with excitement. This was the only thing he missed about being a beat cop, being in the thick of the action. Racing over to an active crime scene provided a rush of adrenaline he'd only felt on the job.

Not that he didn't understand Charli's worries. Derringer might hold key information to their case, and he'd evidently been very concerned about his own safety. It seemed highly unlikely there was a random break-in during the middle of the day. No, whoever was at Derringer's home, they were there to silence him.

Charli and Matthew had to get there first. Fortunately, they'd been nearby when the call came in.

"Look, there's a car in the drive," Charli practically shouted when they turned onto Derringer's street.

A black Lexus was parked out front. "Is someone in it?" Matthew squinted as they fast approached.

"There is and I think…I think it's a woman."

"Pull up right behind her. Don't give her a chance to bolt."

But Charli had already boxed in the car before Matthew could get the rest of his sentence out.

Matthew had his eyes glued to the figure in the vehicle. Now that they were directly behind her, he could see her head shifting from side to side. She was considering her options, planning a getaway. But there was nowhere to go. With a garage in front of her, and their car behind her, she was trapped.

At least, that was what Matthew thought. But this woman apparently wasn't going down without a fight. Her brake lights flashed on for a moment, and the Lexus squealed as she rapidly reversed. The wheel was turned as far to the right as possible in an attempt to bypass Charli's car.

The maneuver almost worked, but there wasn't enough space between them. The Lexus rammed into the front of their car, sending both Matthew and Charli jolting around. Charli let out a short gasp as the momentum threw her back into her seat.

"You bitch!"

As soon as the car ceased moving, they both hopped out as the Lexus started to lurch forward again.

Nope, not if Matthew had anything to say about it. This needed to end now before they ended up in a road chase with their damaged car.

Matthew sprinted forward, pulling his house keys from his jacket pocket as he moved. On them a window hammer, designed to break auto glass in case of emergency. Generally, that emergency was during an accident so the victim could escape the vehicle, but what worked for exiting a car also worked for getting in.

The second he reached the driver's side, he swung the hammer and shattered the safety glass. The woman screamed. Her hands flew up to her face to protect herself, presenting the perfect opportunity for Matthew to reach for the wheel, pulling it in the opposite direction. The Lexus rolled back more slowly this time, the back of it stopping when it hit Charli's car. There was nowhere to go now, and this woman knew it.

Matthew took a step back and drew his gun, pointing it directly at her head. "Get out of the vehicle with your hands up!"

Charli ran up behind Matthew and yanked the door open. "Do exactly what…" Her command fell as recognition dawned. "Tanya? Tanya Greenwood?"

Matthew readjusted his grip. "Wait, this is Bryce's girlfriend?"

Charli shook off her shock and pulled Tanya to the ground, searching her body for any weapons. "One of them."

A shout came from inside the house. Shit.

Charli turned to Matthew, clearly torn with indecision. If they'd had a patrol car, she could simply stuff the girl inside. She looked around and began dragging Tanya toward an ornate streetlamp. She was going to cuff her hands behind her back, securing her to the post.

"Go! I'm right behind you."

But Matthew didn't need permission. He was already sprinting toward the front door. The door was cracked, so Matthew forcefully kicked it in before moving to the side. The more intimidation he came in with, the better.

When no shots were fired, he swung into the room, gun up and ready. Foyer was clear.

"Police! Come out with your hands up!" Matthew shouted, though he was sure nobody would come sprinting toward the door. If Tanya's accomplice was anything like her, he'd bolt. Still, Matthew hoped shuffling feet in the house would guide him to the perpetrator.

There were no shuffling feet. But a voice did ring out.

. . .

"No, please, you don't have to do this! I didn't tell them anything, I swear!"

Matthew moved toward the narrow hallway and turkey-peeked around the first door. There they were. Two men. One bleeding from the leg and crying. The other behind him, a gun raised to his captive's head.

"Help me," the man he recognized as Jack Derringer pleaded.

"Shut up!"

Sweat ran down Aaron Eldridge's face, but the man didn't look scared. He looked excited.

"Police," Matthew called in his command voice. "Drop your weapon, son. You don't want to do this."

Eldridge laughed and pressed the gun harder against Derringer's temple. Then he did something Matthew didn't expect. In the blink of an eye, the gun shifted and Matthew was looking down its cold barrel.

Matthew dove to the side just as the gun kicked in Eldridge's hand. The blast came a second later, and Matthew rolled, raised his own weapon to site Eldridge in.

The man was gone.

The victim dropped to the floor, his leg giving out on him without the extra support. "He shot me."

That much was clear, but it didn't look like a fatal wound, and Matthew could hear sirens growing closer. He needed to find Eldridge.

"Help's on the way." He bolted toward the back of the house, gun raised and ready.

He wasn't going to let that bastard get away.

35

Charli had never wanted to pistol whip anyone as badly as she wanted to whip Tanya Greenwood. The girl's adrenaline had kicked in, and she fought Charli all the way to the street post.

"I swear to god I'll shoot you if you don't stop fighting." Charli yanked one of the girl's arms behind her back. And where the hell was their backup? She could hear sirens but no lights just yet.

"Let me go. He'll kill me. Don't you understand?"

Charli yanked the other arm behind her back. "No, but I will if you don't stop struggling."

Finally, the cuffs clicked into place, and Charli sat back on her heels.

"Please, you've got to—"

Bam.

Oh no, oh no, oh no! Not Matthew. Please let him be okay.

Charli whirled toward the house, leaving Tanya screaming behind her.

Charli's heart drummed in her chest as a fresh dump of

adrenaline surged through her veins.

This was a fear she'd felt before, when she saw Madeline hauled away in that van. She'd never forget those last few seconds. Madeline being stuffed into the back of that vehicle while Charli remained frozen where she stood. Not for long, only a few seconds, but a few seconds was all it'd taken. When Charli got her feet to move, it'd been too late. She could only chase after a van that eventually turned a corner and disappeared.

She couldn't freeze up like that now, not when Matthew needed her.

Charli knew she should secure the perimeter, but having Matthew's back took priority. She pulled her gun from her holster before bursting through the doorway. She rounded the corner just in time to see her partner dart through the back door.

He was alive and moving. Relief almost made her dizzy, but she shook the sensation away.

A man was sprawled on the floor, blood gushing from a wound. The sirens gained more strength. "Help's on the way," she told the writhing man and rushed from the room, turning back the way she'd come.

If Matthew had the back, she'd take the front.

She would get the bastard. He'd shot Derringer and fired at her partner. He wasn't going to get away. Not if she had anything to say about it.

Charli rounded the side of the house in time to spot Eldridge jumping the backyard fence. He stumbled and nearly fell. The gun hit the ground, and he wasted a few precious seconds to turn around and pick it up.

"Don't do it." Her voice was close to a roar as she flew across the yard. She might be small, but she was fast. And she was gaining ground.

To her right, Matthew appeared, and he shouted the same

command.

Eldridge bobbled the gun.

Closer.

His weapon was in his hand, and he was bringing it up. The gun was inches from Charli's head when she put all her weight on her front foot and barreled forward, tackling him to the ground.

Their bodies crashed together, and his gun fell into the grass. Underneath Charli, he reached for it, attempted to crawl under her weight. He could only pull himself a few inches forward before Charli had her gun on the back of his head.

"Stop moving! Touch the gun and I end this!"

The cold barrel pressed against his scalp ended his squirming. He froze. His only movement was the harsh rise and fall of his chest.

"You've got the wrong guy. You don't understand!"

Charli pressed his face in the ground, wishing there was some poison oak nestled within the grass.

"Aaron Eldridge, I'm placing you under arrest." She reached for a pair of handcuffs before remembering she'd already secured one suspect already.

A shiny set appeared beside her. Matthew was there, and he worked Eldridge's arms behind his back while Charli cuffed him.

"This is one big misunderstanding!"

Did he really think that was going to work?

"Yeah, yeah, yeah. Tell it to the stainless steel toilet you'll be using for the rest of your miserable life."

Matthew kicked Eldridge's gun farther from reach. "Jesus, Charli, what were you thinking?"

"I was thinking this monster doesn't get to kill two people, shoot at you, and get away with it."

Matthew grabbed Eldridge by his cuffed hands, and for a

moment, Charli thought she saw a peek of a smile on her partner's face. Was he proud of her?

"Please, you've got to understand!" Eldridge bawled as Matthew pushed his body forward.

"Aaron Eldridge, you're under arrest for the attempted murder of Jack Derringer, for starters." Matthew went through the entire Miranda statement as he escorted him to the front of the house.

"Oh, don't worry, he can afford one." Charli interrupted when Matthew got to the part about a lawyer. "Heard you just made a few million on that pretty little riverfront property you sold."

Eldridge blubbered. "It's not like that. It's—"

"Save your strength, Mr. Eldridge." Charli's voice lilted as she trudged alongside Matthew and their captive. "You'll need it when we get to the precinct. We have so many questions for you."

Charli eagerly awaited that moment. Her mind was running wild with questions because, though they'd caught Eldridge red-handed, this still didn't make complete sense. Why had he taken a shot at Derringer and a detective? What did he have to gain? The kid had just inherited millions of dollars. One would think that being newly wealthy would keep him occupied for a while.

Derringer's driveway and parts of his front yard were filled with cop cars. Paramedics loaded an unconscious Derringer into the back of an ambulance on a stretcher. Charli silently hoped he would be okay.

Matthew and Charli each had a hand on Eldridge, guiding him by his shoulders. They took him to the nearest police vehicle, forcing him into the back seat. Matthew slammed the door and his hulking frame towered over the car as Eldridge began sobbing like a baby.

One of the beat cops, Officer Thomas, flagged Charli down.

"The woman you cuffed is in my car. She wouldn't give a name."

"It's Tanya Greenwood. Please take her down to the station. We have a lot of questions for these two."

36

C harli stared into the one-way mirror. A water bottle sat untouched in front of Eldridge. If he wanted to dehydrate from all his crying, that was his choice.

It was bizarre, to think this shell of a man had attempted to murder someone and was possibly responsible for two other murders. Most people outside law enforcement would think someone who could steal a life would have the fortitude not to fall apart like this.

But it wasn't that unusual, really. Charli had seen "tough guys" fall apart quicker than she could Mirandize them. From what Charli had read, serial killers like John Wayne Gacy were able to go through an interrogation without batting an eye, but they were true sociopaths. Compare them to a run-of-the-mill murderer—god help her that there were such people—who went on a killing spree, and you had a different outcome. This difference set apart the sociopaths from the narcissists. Sociopaths felt nothing while narcissists felt something but only for themselves.

Charli was positive Eldridge wasn't crying like this over Bryce or Chester's bodies. It made the whole scene that much more despicable. Those tears were not for the lives he'd stolen, but merely because he got caught. He was weak.

Despite all the pent-up emotion, though, Charli was doubtful he'd crack. He would cry, for sure, but he hadn't said a word of explanation since they arrived. She was fairly positive that if they asked him anything, he'd only continue to sob. Or ask for an attorney. She was surprised he hadn't done that all ready.

Charli stepped out of Eldridge's observation room and into the one next-door, where another window allowed her to look at Tanya. There were no more tears in her eyes. Had that only been for show? She was sipping her water now and again, looking around the room in what appeared to be abject curiosity. Tanya might actually be a sociopath. Hell, maybe she was the brains of the operation.

A less experienced detective might think that Aaron Eldridge would provide more information, but Charli wasn't so sure. Tanya seemed smart, calculated, like she'd be prepared for this moment. Like she believed she was smarter than everyone else. She was overconfident and Charli could use that to her advantage. Lure Tanya into divulging the truth with a few skillful interview tactics.

One of those tricks she'd learned involved getting some dirt on Tanya. That was where Eldridge could be more useful.

Charli paced between the rooms, adrenaline coursing through her veins. She was eager to start interrogating these two, the plan already forming in her mind. Her focus was interrupted when Matthew stepped into the observation room.

"Charli, Ruth is waiting for us."

Eldridge and Tanya had already been sitting for forty minutes, but they'd have to wait a bit longer. Letting the suspects stew usually helped them crack once the questioning began. If Ruth wanted to be briefed and create a plan before they talked to either of them, then the two entitled folks could cool their heels a little while longer. The more tired and uncomfortable they grew, the more malleable they'd become.

Charli followed Matthew into Ruth's office. A grin was plastered on her face, and it felt weirdly out of place. It was supposed to be welcoming, but she'd seen Ruth smile so seldom, it felt like when a tiger showed its teeth. It was more threatening than anything.

"Very nice work, Detectives. I'm thoroughly impressed. I expect a lot of you two, but even I never expected you'd finish this case up so quickly."

Charli didn't, either. And she didn't feel it was finished yet. There was still a lot they needed to learn.

She smiled her thanks. "How's Derringer? Have you heard how he's doing?"

"He's in surgery, but they're expecting a full recovery, barring any complications. Good news for us, since his testimony will be vital once we throw this case to the prosecutor."

Charli couldn't blame Ruth for thinking this way. It was a hazard of the job. Victim testimony was usually as good as gold. But Charli didn't want Derringer safe because he'd make a good witness. She wanted him to survive for his own well-being.

"Charli is being awfully modest here." Matthew beamed his oafish smile down at Charli as he tugged at his earlobe. "She sprang into action before she had a clue what she was up against. The officers hadn't arrived yet. We might not have caught him if she hadn't tackled the armed suspect as he attempted to flee."

"Truly fantastic work, Detective Cross. But let's focus on the task at hand." Ruth wasn't one to throw out praise any longer than necessary. "What do you know about Eldridge's motive?"

Matthew shrugged. "We've got nothing yet. Derringer might have some insight, but I didn't really have time to ask him as he bled out on the carpet."

"Plan of action?" Ruth looked at Matthew.

This wasn't his forte. Matthew didn't care for psychological profiling and rarely utilized it during interrogations unless he was following Charli's lead.

Charli didn't want to hurt Matthew's feelings, but she knew she was more skilled at dragging information out of a perp. Their eyes met, and Matthew gave her a small nod.

Charli cleared her throat. "I want to dig into Eldridge first. I don't think he's going to tell us anything about why he did it, but he may provide solid information on Tanya and her involvement. Once I have that, maybe I can manipulate Tanya into telling the truth."

Ruth nodded. "Yes, good. That's a solid plan. Remember, you two, the dirty work may be done, but now the real work begins. It's all eyes on us right now. Do we know yet how these two know each other? What they each had to gain from working together?"

Matthew raised a shoulder. "Not a clue...yet."

Ruth raised an eyebrow. "Well, then I guess you two need to go find out."

37

Charli expected Aaron would still be crying when they entered the room. But she wasn't expecting his screams to escalate to ear-piecing as soon as he heard the door open.

He was embellishing. It wasn't the first time Charli had seen the behavior. But she never understood it. It took a truly daft narcissist to think anyone was going to empathize with a killer just because he cried.

She rolled her eyes at Matthew.

He responded by slamming his notebook onto the table, jolting Aaron's head up. "Did Chester or Bryce cry like that while you were killing them?"

Aaron's tears slowed. They didn't cease entirely, but he stopped gasping for air like a salmon scooped out of the stream by a starving bear. The message from Matthew had been well understood. He wasn't going to be getting any empathy from them after what he'd done.

But Aaron didn't answer. He wasn't stupid enough to admit fault. Charli expected this, and she wasn't counting on it. Still, they planned to ask a few questions about the crime scene to soften him up for the information they actually wanted.

"Aaron, what reason did you have to go after Bryce?" Charli glanced down at her notebook casually.

"None. I didn't have any reason. And I wouldn't do that."

"What about Chester?" Matthew followed up.

"Chester bought my land. He treated me like a friend. He was a good guy."

"Oh, come on, now." Matthew grinned at him. "You don't have to lie. We know Chester wasn't a good guy. Everyone and their mother complained about what an asshole he was. I'm sure if you did kill him, he deserved it."

Aaron wasn't tripped up by this comment, and Charli knew he wouldn't be. But using overtly manipulative statements about the murders would cause Aaron to think they were desperate.

"I liked Chester just fine." Aaron sat up straighter in his chair, wiping his eyes. "I was devastated when I heard he was dead."

"Do you really expect us to believe that?" Matthew moved his head forward, his gaze taunting Aaron. "You shot at me. You went to Derringer's house to kill him. And you expect me to believe you're sympathetic to Bryce and Chester's deaths? You had nothing to do with them?"

Matthew was so good at playing bad cop, Charli would never be able to compete with his act. She'd love to switch roles one time for the hell of it, but her round cheeks and youthful appearance would never look as intimidating.

"I am sympathetic. I was friends with both Bryce and Chester."

"Huh. That's weird because Tanya told us the opposite." Charli kept her tone approachable.

Though Eldridge was doing a pretty good job of keeping

his expression neutral, his eye twitched at the corner. "You spoke to Tanya already?"

Charli widened her eyes. "You didn't know that? I would've told you, but I assumed you knew why it took us so long to get in here."

It was a lie, but Eldridge bought it hook, line, and sinker. Outside of physical intimidation, there weren't many rules about what could or couldn't be said during an investigation. It was completely within Charli's rights to lie to a perp to draw out a confession.

"She's a lying bitch!" Eldridge slammed his hands down.

Good, so Tanya was a sore spot. It wouldn't be hard to get what Charli needed.

"What makes you say that?" Charli tapped her pen against the table.

"Did she tell you she was fucking all of us?" Spittle sprayed from Eldridge's mouth. "Not just me, not just Bryce, but Chester too."

Under the table, Charli nudged Matthew's foot. It was her way of telling him he needed to pull out the bad cop again.

"Seriously? Eldridge, you sound like a jealous boyfriend. Sure you're not trying to defame her to make yourself look better? We see this kind of thing all the time. As soon as a couple is dragged into custody, the boyfriend claims his lady is a lying, cheating whore."

"I am not her fucking boyfriend. And she is a whore."

"How would you even know this? Sure, you could know about her history with Bryce." Matthew's laugh almost sounded demonic. "But you expect me to believe she straight up told you she was screwing Chester?"

Aaron's eyes shifted. "I found out myself. Her phone number came up on Chester's phone once when..." He slammed his mouth shut, nostrils flaring. After taking a deep breath, he looked calmer. "Like I was saying, her number came up on Chester's phone when he and I were together, so I knew she was a cheating whore."

An obvious lie. But Charli wasn't expecting the truth, so she didn't bother to call it out.

This was the game that had to be played with perps sometimes. You take the truth that you can get. Aaron wouldn't admit to any crime, but not everything that came out of his mouth would be a lie. And this hatred for Tanya would be the most honest thing to come from him.

Charli rested her chin on her fist. "If she wasn't your girlfriend, why exactly do you care?"

"It's not about her belonging to me. I don't care who she screws. She could fuck the whole town and I wouldn't bat an eye if she was hooking up with people out of real desire. But look at the men she goes for." He stuck out his tongue like he was gagging. "Bryce, Chester, and I only have one thing in common."

"And what thing is that?" Matthew deadpanned. "It sure isn't devilish good looks."

Eldridge huffed for a second but moved on from the comment. "Our money. Tanya was hedging her bets. Women like that are the scum of the earth. She wanted to end up with a rich guy, and she was going to do anything she could to make sure that happened."

"Even...help you?" Matthew's expression was like a glacial mask.

Aaron's eyes darted between the detectives, but he remained quiet.

Charli dug a little further. "Are you telling me you had no idea Tanya was seeing Chester? She didn't do that because it was part of your plan to lure him in?"

"No!" Aaron's response rushed from his mouth. "No. I didn't lure him in. And I definitely didn't suggest Tanya should be involved with Chester."

Charli believed part of it. All that crap Tanya had given her about being forced into this, it didn't vibe with how she was acting now. She had seemed unfazed awaiting the detectives to question her.

If she was actually a victim in this situation, she wouldn't expect Tanya to show such peace of mind. And her motive made sense. As unhinged as Eldridge was, Charli didn't disagree that Tanya could have been seducing all these men for the financial gain. She wasn't well off herself. She even admitted to Charli that she put up with Bryce's cheating because she was attracted to his lifestyle.

It didn't answer the question about Aaron's motives, however. He already had millions of dollars. Not that being wealthy ever stopped anyone from wanting to attain more wealth. The billionaires of the world proved no amount of cash would stop someone from seeking more. But killing Bryce and Chester didn't appear to provide Eldridge with additional money.

Charli could be patient, though. If Eldridge was able to provide them with Tanya's motive, perhaps Tanya could provide them with Aaron's.

38

Through the one-way mirror, Tanya sat stoic, her posture upright and her gaze centered on the wall in front of her. But as soon as the door cracked, she began to sniffle and wipe her hand across her eyes. There were no real tears, but she wouldn't miss an opportunity to make it appear there had been.

"We've got a few questions, Tanya." Matthew dragged his chair along the tile, causing a disconcerting screech to emanate from the chair legs.

The girl winced but managed to keep her puppy dog expression in place. "You have to believe me. I didn't want to do any of this. I was in love with Bryce, and I didn't even know Chester."

Well, Tanya certainly didn't intend to be honest.

Charli shrugged. "That isn't what your buddy Aaron said."

Tanya's lips tightened. "What did Aaron tell you?"

"Oh, just that you had been screwing both Bryce and Chester."

Her jaw dropped. The shock on her face was the first

genuine emotion Charli had seen since they apprehended her.

Charli was starting to enjoy this. "You didn't know that he knew, did you? About Chester?"

Aaron may have actually been right. There was something to his jealousy. Tanya may have been playing all three of them, intending to stick it out with whoever ended up rich and victorious.

"I don't know what you're talking about. I never dated Chester."

"You sure about that?" Matthew leaned forward. "Because we're going to go through Chester's phone records. And if your name pops up, it's going to be pretty suspicious that you told us you never knew the man."

The sad eyes Tanya had thrown on when they entered the room disappeared. It wasn't going to be so easy to feign ignorance now.

"Then what are you doing here?" Tanya's voice was almost a hiss. She had become a cornered cat. Her only defense now was to strike back.

"What do you mean?" Charli leaned back casually.

"I mean, if you're going to check the phone records, go do that. If you have incriminating evidence of me, fine. Do what you're going to do. I can't stop it now, so why would I talk to you?"

Charli wanted to shake the woman. "You can't change the evidence we're going to find, that's true. But that doesn't mean you can't be helpful to this investigation. Your compliance will go a long way. We help people who help us."

Tanya wasn't buying it. She turned her head to the mirror, putting her face in her hand. Her hair fell across her shoulders, and she twirled a lock on the tip of her finger.

"I've never been great at compliance."

Matthew slammed his fist onto the table, causing Tanya to shoot up in her chair.

"Do you get what is on the line here? Your entire life. Right now, the only ones who know what really happened are you and Eldridge. And let me tell you, that man isn't interested in doing you any favors. The person who comes out on top here is the one who can convince us, and the county prosecutor, that they didn't come up with this plan. Eldridge is going to do whatever he can to pin it on you. You must know there is no loyalty in the interrogation room."

Tanya bit her lip. "Maybe there is. I know you cops do this. You try to make it seem like one person is flipping on the other so they'll cave. Maybe Aaron is loyal to me. He seemed loyal to me yesterday."

"If he was loyal to you, how do we know about Chester?" Charli asked point blank.

Tanya opened her mouth and then closed it. She didn't have an answer.

Matthew chuckled to himself before folding his arms. "I actually think we did you a favor by catching you today. Because that psycho over there, he hates your guts. He's a cold-blooded killer, and he doesn't care for you. If he convinced you he cared for you, then you were being played. After whatever you pulled with Chester, Aaron wants nothing to do with you."

Tanya's eyes drifted to the table. She knew it to be true. Tanya hadn't a clue that Aaron ever knew about Chester. That changed things. Her act had fallen apart, and her only audience now was Charli and Matthew.

"If I talk to you, will you be able to help me out? You know, with my case?"

The smallest of smiles tweaked at Matthew's lips. "I'm sure something can be arranged."

Tanya let out a long sigh. "What do you want to know?"

"Everything." Charli pulled out her pen.

"What do I get in return?"

Charli nearly punched the wall. She was so sick of criminals trying to trade favors for information, but that was how the system worked.

"I'm sure the prosecutor's office will take your testimony into consideration if you help us create a solid case."

Tanya crossed her arms. "I'd like that in writing."

Matthew groaned beside her, and the two of them left the room. An hour later, the agreement had been sighed. The prosecutor had agreed to leniency if Tanya cooperated.

Back at the table, Charli opened her notebook again. "Talk."

Tanya was silent for a moment. She rubbed her eyes and began to do just that. "As soon as Aaron inherited that strip of land from his uncle, he knew he was going to sell it. Developers offered buckets of money for property along the Ogeechee River, but Chester offered the most. His bid blew everyone else out of the water, but his plans were lacking. He wanted to put another luxury hotel up, like Savannah didn't have enough of those."

Charli and Matthew eyed each other, but it was Matthew who spoke. "Wait, why would that matter? Once Aaron got his money, why would he care what happened to the land?"

Tanya gave an arrogant smile. "Detective, have you not met the rich assholes in this town? Aaron didn't grow up with money, but he had a whole lot of jealousy. If envy translated into cash, Aaron would already be the richest man in Savannah. So, when he was on the brink of getting a windfall, it wasn't enough to walk away with millions. He wanted this to be his big break, to run with the big dogs. When he saw Bryce's plan for an open-air mall, he saw the opportunity to make millions annually in passive income. The only barrier was, of course, that Bryce's name was attached to it."

"So…Aaron killed him for it?" Charli thought that motive was a little thin. "But how would killing Bryce transfer ownership over to Aaron?"

"Bryce only had partial ownership of that plan. He'd been working with a designer in New York. Aaron met with him and convinced him to sell Aaron his stake. Of course, Aaron had to make sure that nobody else knew about Bryce's share in the plan. He had to align with somebody close to him to find that out."

"And that was you?" Charli saw pride in Tanya's eyes. There was no regret about betraying Bryce, not an ounce of shame.

"I told him nobody knew about those plans except the folks Bryce was working with in New York and myself. If Bryce were to unexpectedly disappear, nobody else would show up to claim the blueprints. And I directed him to the contact information of Bryce's associate in New York. Bryce liked to talk about himself a lot. I was the only one he told about his business. He was too afraid to tell his friends or family, in case he failed." Tanya shrugged.

"So, you knew Eldridge wanted Bryce dead?" Matthew's disgust at Tanya's lack of remorse was etched into his features.

"Not then." She rolled her eyes. "Aaron didn't want Bryce dead until he learned about the salamanders."

Charli blinked. "Excuse me?"

She rolled her eyes again. "Apparently, there is some rare, almost extinct salamander that lives on the land Aaron was selling."

Charli had a feeling she knew where this was going.

"From the environmental study?"

Tanya nodded. "Yeah. I don't know all the laws and shit, but from what Aaron told me, the EPA was going to declare a big chunk of his land as a sanctuary for those gross little things. Can you imagine?"

Actually, Charli could.

"I've read all the paperwork for the sale of that land." Charli pulled a thick packet from a folder she'd brought with her. "There is no mention of salamanders."

Tanya smiled. "That's because Aaron bribed the EPA dude. He wasn't going to let some reptiles get in his way of millions."

"Amphibians," Charli corrected.

Tanya tilted her head. "Huh?"

Charli waved a hand. "Never mind. Let's go back. I'm guessing that Crabtree ordered the EPA study before buying the land." At Tanya's nod, she glanced at the camera recording their every word. "For the record, Miss Greenwood nodded the affirmative to that question. Then, Aaron somehow learned of the salamanders' presence and bribed the EPA inspector to make the problem go away?"

Another nod. "Yes."

Tanya was a fast learner. Too bad she was also selfish and stupid.

"What happened after that?"

"Well, someone at the EPA apparently found out the incorrect findings, but the dude Aaron bribed managed to give Aaron a heads-up."

Charli's stomach churned. "What did Aaron do next?"

"Well, like I said, he couldn't let an…amphibian get in his way of millions, so he learned the whistleblower's name and," she shrugged, "took care of him."

Another murder. Charli shouldn't have been surprised. She'd circle back to those details in a moment. First, she needed to know more.

"Why Bryce?"

Tanya's eyes brightened, and she leaned forward, almost

like she was about to spill some juicy gossip. "Well, he'd told Bryce about the problem with the little creatures, thinking that Bryce would be as upset as him. But he wasn't. Bryce was pissed that he'd choose money over the environment, which really surprised Aaron. Aaron was mad but was also afraid that Bryce would run his mouth."

"So, Aaron killed him, making the death look like a suicide."

Tanya nodded. "Yes."

Bryce Mowery, playboy extraordinaire, was killed because he defended the lives of salamanders. Who would have thunk it?

Charli wanted to ask the girl what role she played in the murder, but she wanted her to finish her story first.

"And Chester Crabtree?"

Tanya spread her hands. "Do I even need to say it? Aaron knew that if Chester found out, the sale would be null and void. He couldn't let that happen now, could he?" She inspected her fingernails. "And for the record, Aaron wanted me to play nice with Chester so I could tell him of Chester's whereabouts."

Well, Aaron clearly hadn't considered "playing nice" to mean for his girlfriend to sleep with the man, but good grief. What had the asshole really expected?

Charli sighed, disappointed in humanity and a bit embarrassed to be part of the human race. She gave herself a mental shake and refocused on her questions. "What about Jack Derringer?"

"Well, I'm not so sure how Jack learned about the false EPA study, but you know how people talk." She waved a hand. "Aaron was going to leave for Mexico but decided to stop by Jack's house first and take care of him." She pressed her lips together. "He wouldn't listen to me. I told him we just needed to go."

Did this young woman not understand that she was probably the next victim on Aaron's list?

Probably not.

This woman was ruthless, perhaps even more so than
Aaron Eldridge. According to her, she didn't come up with
the plan, but she had no second thoughts about involving
herself. For her, these men were only a means to an end,
nothing more.

Matthew took a sip of water from the bottle he'd brought
in with him. "How did your involvement in all of this begin?"

She shrugged. "It started because I liked nice things, and
going out with the rich guys is better than dating the poor
ones."

Matthew opened his mouth, but Charli pressed her knee
against his leg. She wanted him to stay quiet and let Tanya
talk as much as she wanted to.

"Aaron was good to me. Chester too. He was actually
going to take me out to dinner when he was killed. We'd just
finished making love in his office, and I was cleaning up." She
shuddered. "I could have been with him in that garage. Aaron
doesn't know that part."

He'd learn about it soon enough.

"What about Bryce?"

Another shrug. "He was okay, I guess. Fun. Kind of excit-
ing. But I knew he'd never be faithful in the way that would
protect me long-term." She rubbed her belly, and Charli's
mouth dropped open. Tanya smiled. "Yeah. I'm about six
weeks along."

Fury ran through Charli's veins.

"Who's the father?"

Tanya continued to stroke her flat stomach. "Does it
really matter?"

There was a hollowness to Tanya, no emotion in her
voice. Charli could understand growing up poor and

wanting more for yourself. She even understood hating Savannah's upper class. But she'd never understand how any woman utilized her womanhood to use and then eliminate men without remorse.

Bryce and Chester weren't good men, but that didn't mean they deserved such brutal deaths. And the EPA agent. That was a whole different investigation.

And to bring a baby into the picture? The poor child.

Charli needed a break from her. This level of dark greed made her sick to her stomach.

After the last investigation, she was physically and mentally exhausted. And they'd gotten the information they needed. It was time to step aside and regroup. She, Matthew, and Ruth could convene and decide what further questions needed to be asked.

She nearly groaned when she pushed to her feet. Tanya's eyes widened. "Where are you going?"

Charli met the young woman's gaze. "Anywhere away from you."

39

"We are deeply saddened by the tragic loss of both Bryce Mowery and Chester Crabtree, but we can assure the community that the people responsible have been apprehended and will stand trial. This would not have been possible without the diligent work of Detective Cross and Detective Church." Ruth finished her speech with confidence, her head swaying slightly from left to right as she read from her cue cards on the podium.

Matthew had his hands behind his back but used his elbow to nudge Charli. She looked up to find him smiling at her, a glimmer in his eyes. He was proud of her, and she was proud of herself. But that pride shrank a bit against the limelight of all the reporters surrounding them.

Charli found herself actually hoping she didn't get another high-profile case any time soon. Not that she didn't love the challenge of solving the case, but she couldn't handle another round of media attention. At least she only had to stand off to the side next to Matthew. Ruth had promised she wouldn't have to open her mouth.

"I'll now take any questions." Ruth stood up straighter behind the podium.

Charli hated this part in particular. At least she knew everything Ruth was going to say, but questions were a curveball, and occasionally, a reporter would try to throw a question to the detectives. Charli hated to fumble her words on local television. She was normally so careful with her words, able to navigate an interrogation with eagle-eyed precision. Put a camera in her face, though, and intelligible language left her.

"What was Eldridge's motive to kill Mowery and Crabtree?" A male reporter in a navy blue business suit raised his hand.

"We can't get into specifics right now, but I will say that the motive was financial. We don't believe the general public was ever in danger."

"And Eldridge has now confessed to the crimes?" the same reporter asked.

"He has plead guilty, yes."

After they told Eldridge everything they'd learned from his lover, Eldridge knew he would face significant jail time. He hired an elite law firm to represent him and was advised to accept the plea deal. He and his lawyer were still negotiating a way to keep him out of jail for the rest of his life, while the prosecution was currently only willing to take the death penalty off the table.

But he admitted to everything that Tanya hadn't been able to confirm. He killed three people and wounded another. And that was just the beginning of the long list of charges against the man.

It was an open and shut case now, but the success didn't take away from the emptiness growing within Charli. She had been around a lot of death over the past few weeks, and solving a case didn't take away from lives lost. This played a big role in her distaste for the limelight. She didn't need any more praise. It wouldn't bring back the lives that had been taken.

Thankfully, the press conference ended a short time later, and Charli and Matthew were able to exit into the precinct. Ruth followed them in, patting them both on the backs but saying nothing before exiting to her office.

Matthew turned to Charli. "So, don't think we've got much work left today. You wanna…" He looked over her shoulder.

"What?" Charli turned around to see what had caught his attention.

Preston Powell stood behind her, a small smile plastered on his cheeks. Matthew still didn't care much for the GBI agent who had helped them on their last case, so he scurried down the hall without another word.

Charli didn't share the animosity. She thought highly of Preston after working with him.

"It would seem fame and notoriety follow you, Detective Cross."

"Yes, well, I assure you that I run for the shadows as much as possible." Charli tried to cover the exasperation she felt about her unwanted fame.

"Can't blame them for following you. Your work has been thoroughly impressive. And you look good on camera."

Wait, was he…hitting on her?

Charli hardly knew how to reply. It'd been a long time since anyone flirted with her. And she'd never been good at accepting compliments on her physical appearance. Offer positive feedback on her work performance, great. But she put zero effort into her appearance, so it felt weird to accept compliments on what she was merely born with.

"Uh, thanks." The words came out quieter than she intended, but it didn't appear to bother Preston.

"I was hoping to run into you. I'm in town for the next few weeks on a narcotics ring case. As soon as I was assigned to it, I thought I might finally get the opportunity to ask you to dinner." He shifted a bit, sliding his hands into his pockets.

Charli's mouth fell ajar for just a second before she realized and tightened it back up. "To dinner?"

"Yes. I figured I should ask now, before you continue to grow more popular. Don't want you thinking I'm just some crazed fan."

He was quick, and if he wasn't asking her out, Charli would be able to respond with equal wit. But just like the cameras, his request for a date had left her speechless.

And after all the chaos of the last few cases, Charli didn't know how to begin to consider the offer. With everything weighing heavy on her heart, was this the time for dating?

Or perhaps that was exactly why she needed to say yes. Charli was inundated with the memories of many lonely nights, her caseloads imbedded in her brain without anyone to discuss them with. She'd avoided social relationships for so long, Matthew being her only real friend. How long could she go on like that?

Hadn't she punished herself long enough for Madeline's death? She'd dropped out of life after her murder, focusing on nothing but the dream of becoming a homicide investigator and finding Madeline's killer. She'd succeeded in the detective part, and she was damn good at it. But she wouldn't rest until she found the man responsible for her best friend's death.

Ultimately, Charli decided Madeline would have pushed her to accept the invitation, no matter how uncomfortable it made her.

"Sure." When the word came out, it sounded foreign. It was too chipper, containing an optimism Charli didn't know was within her.

"Great! How about this Friday night?"

Breathe in. Breathe out.

Charli gazed up into his handsome face, and a weird fluttery little thing started churning in her stomach. "It's a date. You've got my number. Call me with the details."

"Will do."

As Charli walked away, she did her best to conceal her heavy breathing. After agreeing, a wave of panic set in. What had she just done?

Despite her fears, the corners of her lips turned up as she walked to her office.

The smile didn't last very long, though, because Ruth appeared in her doorway just as she and Matthew were about to call it a night.

Charli groaned. "Please tell me we don't have to meet with any more reporters."

"You do not. Though I hope you'll both read the *Savannah Journal* article on the Eldridge case tomorrow. You two, and the rest of the department, will be painted in a very positive light. You're becoming the faces of Savannah PD."

Matthew beamed while Charli dropped her face in her hands. "Do not remind me."

Ruth's chuckle only lasted a second. "I need to take advantage of the hot streak you two are on."

Matthew and Charli exchanged weary glances. "Does that mean you've got another case for us?"

"I do."

Through her exhaustion, fresh excitement sparked to life. Charli grabbed her notepad. "What is it?"

Ruth grinned. "Do either of you believe in voodoo?"

The End
To be continued...

Thank you for reading.
All of the *Charli Cross Series* books can be found on Amazon.

ACKNOWLEDGMENTS

How does one properly thank everyone involved in taking a dream and making it a reality? Here goes.

In addition to our families, whose unending support provided the foundation for us to find the time and energy to put these thoughts on paper, we want to thank the editors who polished our words and made them shine.

Many thanks to our publisher for risking taking on two newbies and giving us the confidence to become bona fide authors.

More than anyone, we want to thank you, our readers, for clicking on a couple of nobodies and sharing your most important asset, your time, with this book. We hope with all our hearts we made it worthwhile.

Much love,

Mary & Donna

ABOUT THE AUTHOR

Mary Stone

Mary Stone lives among the majestic Blue Ridge Mountains of East Tennessee with her two dogs, four cats, a couple of energetic boys, and a very patient husband.

As a young girl, she would go to bed every night, wondering what type of creature might be lurking underneath. It wasn't until she was older that she learned that the creatures she needed to most fear were human.

Today, she creates vivid stories with courageous, strong heroines and dastardly villains. She invites you to enter her world of serial killers, FBI agents but never damsels in distress. Her female characters can handle themselves, going toe-to-toe with any male character, protagonist or antagonist.

Discover more about Mary Stone on her website.
www.authormarystone.com

Donna Berdel

Raised as an Army brat, Donna has lived all over the world, but no place has given her as much peace as the home she lives in with her husband near Myrtle Beach. But while she now keeps her feet planted firmly in the sand, her mind goes back to those cities and the people she met and said goodbye to so many times.

With her two adopted cats fighting for lap space, she brings those she loved (and those she didn't) back as characters in her books. And yes, it's kind of fun to kill off anyone who was mean to her in the past. Mean clerk at the grocery store...beware!

Connect with Mary Online

facebook.com/authormarystone
goodreads.com/AuthorMaryStone
bookbub.com/profile/3378576590
pinterest.com/MaryStoneAuthor

Printed in Great Britain
by Amazon